A.L. Williams is a prolific writer of both stories and songs. In 1985, his sweetheart, Kathy Ratzburg, and he started a band called One Lane Bridge to showcase their original music.

A.L. Williams had always been interested in the saga of John Dillinger. Intrigued by the theory that Dillinger was not the man killed in Chicago by the FBI, he began two years of research into the subject. At a book signing he told Vickie Weaver, a high-school classmate and published author, of this research. Vickie encouraged him to write a book about it. His first effort, Hey There, Johnny Dillinger, was never published, but it did get him interested in the art and magic of writing books.

Finally in 2021 his very dark story, *Satan's Guitar*, garnered the attention of and was accepted by the publisher Austin Macauley for printing.

His debut pits a bass player named Marshall King against the Devil's own evil instrument. A 1963 Gibson ES-335 guitar.

It is not of major importance, but Mr. Williams has shared his life with nine cats and seven dogs.

To: Kathy Ratzburg (RIP) – for putting and keeping my life on track.

To: Vickie Weaver – for her encouragement to start writing books.

To: Caitlin (Kat) Katelynne – for insisting that I complete this story.

To: Winston – for being the best little pal ever.

A.L. Williams

SATAN'S GUITAR

AUSTIN MACAULEY PUBLISHERS™

LONDON • CAMBRIDGE • NEW YORK • SHARJAH

Ordering Information
Quantity sales: Special discounts are available on quantity purchases by corporations, associations, and others. For details, contact the publisher at the address below.

Publisher's Cataloging-in-Publication data
Williams, A. L.
Satan's Guitar

ISBN 9781638298601 (Paperback)
ISBN 9781638298618 (ePub e-book)

Library of Congress Control Number: 2023903473

www.austinmacauley.com/us

First Published 2023
Austin Macauley Publishers LLC
40 Wall Street 33rd Floor, Suite 3302
New York, NY 10005
USA

mail-usa@austinmacauley.com
+1 (646) 5125767

2/5/2013 2:40 pm – 4/8/2019 12:27 am

Warning: Foul Language

I
The Rules

The Adversary's Axe was set free late in the year of 1963. It was a wickedly deep red, semi-hollow bodied Gibson ES-335 guitar.

Lucifer himself played a scorching riff and solo on it, running his long crimson fingers, with nails manicured to perfection, up and down the silky neck.

The possessor of the Hellish instrument could keep it only if they played it every night at midnight, and committed at least one evil deed each day. Things went smoothly as long as these two requirements were honored. If not, well, there would be Hell to pay and the Axe would then seek a new player.

It went without saying that the guitarist's soul was doomed.

It wasn't The Crossroads at midnight and there were no handshakes with the Devil. The deal was never made directly. Instead, it was consummated through unknowing and/or unwilling participants. Their lives were usually destroyed as the guitar made its way from dark soul to dark soul. The guitar's evil essence waxed strong without concern for innocence. As it came to be, there were a great many victims that were innocent.

Satan's Guitar, like all Gibson guitars, was lovingly and painstakingly built. Resonant woods, cured, molded and shaped over a period of years, were fitted together with precision craftsmanship. The ES-335, serial number 63666, was by all standards, a most excellent instrument. It's final factory inspection took place on November 22, 1963.

The inspector entered the model and serial numbers on a line in the shipping log book. The box by the words 'Quality Assured' was checked off. He then placed the Axe into a special velvet lined jet-black case. He noted the recipient's address. It was shipping to a music store in Osgood, Indiana. One of Satan's minions promptly purloined it and dropped it down into Hell.

Beelzebub played that incredible solo just as Lee Harvey Oswald, sighting his mail order rifle from a sixth-floor window at the President's head, gently squeezed the trigger. The riff and solo floated away as the last notes were picked out by Satan's fingers. They would turn up again in a hit rock song.

Behind Him, the band of the day was laying down some supergroove back up music. Buddy Rich was drumming, so things were really tight. Satan loved it when Buddy drummed; the man understood exactly what was needed to make things sizzle and smoke. Mr. Rich wasn't technically dead; in fact, he was very much alive and at the top of his career on Earth. He had traded his soul for his drumming abilities a long time ago, part of the deal being that once in a while he would sit in with his Master's band. When Satan was in the mood for a really righteous jam, he would summon the drummer from the planet's surface to join in and set a vicious tempo.

Buddy's band members noticed that when he returned from one of his short vacations, his chops were vastly improved, leading them to believe that all he did when he was gone was practice, even though he hated to practice. He was also always severely dehydrated, and if possible, a bigger asshole than usual.

Immediately the Devil became bored and tossed the Axe carelessly aside.

One of His tortured souls retrieved the guitar and returned it to the surface for its most deadly mission. Eyes only, ordered straight from Himself at the Bottom.

It wasn't the first instrument He had sent to inflict pain on earth. In 64 A.D., Nero plucked on a lyre also imbedded with evil purpose.

Music was used against Satan as well. God had St. Patrick lead the snakes out of Ireland with a flute just to prove a point.

II
The Beginning

"This is strange, honey."

"What's that, babe?"

"We have an extra guitar here that isn't shown on the shipping manifest."

"Well, that's our address on the label." Sure enough, it was their address on the label, attached with a stretch string to the single handle of the deep black case. One of the shop's purchase order numbers was clearly printed on the tag.

"That's funny," she said, "I'm sure that I deleted that number last month."

"Probably just a shipping mistake," he countered as he lifted the case onto the counter.

She pondered. "How could Gibson get one of our deleted purchase order numbers?"

"I don't know, sweetie, let's take a look at it."

The guitar shop, recently founded by the young husband and wife, was quickly picking up a good reputation. He knew guitars, she knew finance and dealing. They were a natural pair.

The last snap clicked and he carefully opened the top. For a moment he felt as if he were lifting the heavy-hinged lid of a casket.

In front of their eyes, the Axe transformed from a slightly hazy, shifting shape to a solid mass. It was the most vibrant red either of them had ever seen. "Mistake or not, we're keeping this baby," he declared.

She clearly did not like the idea. Sensing the evil, she began shaking her head exclaiming, "No! No! No!" He reached in and ran his thumb across the strings from low to high, the tone was pure and the tuning perfect. As his thumb slide over the high E, a burning pain shot through it. "Ouch! Damn it!"

"Honey, are you alright?"

Violently jerking his hand away, he looked down at the injury. Blood welled up, drawing a straight line of angry, brutal red across the tip. He instinctively stuck the thumb into his mouth, it tasted strongly of sulfate and guitar string cleaner.

A drop of his blood left on the thin string ignited, the flame bursting as sudden as a struck match. Making no sound, the case top dropped solidly back into place.

III
Jason and Jeff

"Just give us the fucking money and no one will get hurt!"

"We don't have much here, we haven't even been to the bank yet today," she pleaded, looking at the long barrel of the silver finished revolver.

"Nobody cares, you bitch! Just give us what you got!" Looking at the pitch back case, Jason demanded, "What is that?"

"It's a guitar. It's very valuable! You can have it. Take it and go!"

"No!" the husband screamed, "Not the guitar!"

"Shut up! Jeff, open that case."

Jeff obeyed his twin brother as he always did, without question. Jason was six hours, six minutes, and six seconds older than Jeff and the Alpha of the pair. This would be the very last order Jeff would take from Jason.

A slight blur at first, it once again took form, Jeff fell in love. He pointed his revolver at the husband and shot him dead.

"Jeff, Jesus Christ! Why in the fuck did you do that?"

"Didn't like him, Jason. Listen, let's have some fun with this here lady."

"Man, this is a fucking beautiful guitar! I'll bet we can get five hundred bucks for it easy!"

Jeff was having none of that. "We're not selling this guitar, Jason, you asshole, it's mine!"

Jason, not used to lip from Jeff, showed his fist. "Don't talk back to me, you stupid motherfucker, I'll beat your brains out! You can't play the guitar anyway, you dumbass."

"I'll learn!"

"Give me a fucking break, when have you ever been able to learn anything?"

Jeff lifted his weapon once more. Not even seeming to aim, he heart-shot Jason and dropped him right on top of the raped and now dead wife.

Rushing out the door with his prize, Jeff never looked back or even thought of his twin brother again. Barely two hours later on 421 South, Jeff was hanging through the windshield of a stolen 1963 Chevy Impala after being stupid enough to run from the Indiana Highway Patrol.

It was only a couple of days after the quality assurance inspector had signed off on the ES-335 and already the Axe was causing havoc in the lives of those unfortunate enough to get within its sphere of influence.

Not finding a player yet, Hell's Master was growing impatient even though He knew the Axe would eventually succeed in locating one. There were a lot of guitarists living on this particular ball of water and dirt, but waiting for the right one, even though unpleasant, was one of God's silly rules.

It was hard for Him to refrain from acting, but Satan had rules to follow. He was only allowed to set the guitar in motion on its evil excursion. He could not direct it, or even know where it was going to wind up next.

The Devil didn't like to play by rules, but he agreed to them as laid out.

Why the hell not? He reasoned to Himself that there would still be plenty of pain and suffering inflicted on those pesky humans.

IV
The First Player

The first real player held onto Satan's Guitar until 1967. It was love at first touch; the impeccably fretted neck just begged to be played. He knew this guitar was going to take him places fast and far. It did.

One year after the Axe found him, Rusty was long gone from the dead-end junkyard job with its piles of crushed automobiles and the giant screaming shredder, nowhere near the bastard slave-driving owner, and far, far away from anything resembling goodness.

As garage bands go, the one Rusty Collins was in at twenty-three, was mediocre at best. He was only an average player himself, but was fueled by a true passion for music.

Then…things changed!

The red hollow-bodied guitar was inside a badly wrecked '63 Chevy that effused a coppery, burnt blood smell.

The state police had ordered the Impala towed to the scrapyard where Rusty worked. Their investigation was completed and it was no longer needed as evidence.

His job was to pick up cars with a giant electromagnet and drop them onto the shredder's conveyor belt. Even though he wore heavy-duty hearing protection, the sound of the metal being ripped apart for hours on end rang loudly in his ears.

The totaled Chevy was next in line for destruction. Rusty walked by it on his return from lunch and took a peek inside.

There it sat, never noticed by the state police or insurance people that poured over the vehicle after the deadly crash. The seat leather on the passenger's side was clean and undamaged. Accident scene photos taken showed it in the shape of a guitar case.

Lying dormant, vibrations slowed to frequencies below human perception, it was waiting for just the right person, a player. Skill level would make little to no difference as long as the soul was for sale. The Axe would ensure incredible playing.

Rusty's first impression of it was as a pile of torn and loose black rags on the passenger seat. He squinted and looked closer as the material took on a more solid appearance. Rusty, quickly realizing that it was a guitar case, reached through the deformed window and pulled it out.

Wondering how everybody that had examined the wreck had missed a guitar, he placed the case on the trunk lid and clicked opened the clasps.

On the rare night that none of his bands were playing a gig, Rusty would hold jam sessions wherever he happened to be. Slowly winding up to a solid wall of sound by the clock stroke of twelve, he would then allow the music to slowly wane into complete silence. Silencio to Crescendo to Silencio.

V

Collateral Damage

Only one person ever complained about the excessive noise in the middle of the night. She was found by the hotel maid the next morning choked to death on an olive from her martini.

One of Rusty's promo guitar picks was found by an investigator lying under the glass from which she had been sipping her elixir of quietude.

The thumb and fingerprint found on it were from a serial killer executed in Texas a few years previously. As a detective on the homicide squad, the investigator was involved in that case and had made a trip to the prison to personally watch the killer die. The homicide detective would spend the rest of his life trying to find any connection between an executed psychopath and the dead lady. He would fail to do so on this side of time.

Denise Williams was having a lousy sixteenth birthday. In home room, thanks to the invention of the alphabet, Alan the louse sat beside her every day at school. This morning, Alan the louse grabbed and snapped in half the Happy Birthday pencil given to her by her little sister.

Later that day, during driver's education class, Coach Teauge announced that if anyone had a weak stomach, they should leave before the film was shown. *Signal Thirty*, produced by the Indiana Highway Patrol, was a way to show new drivers the dire consequences if they failed to properly control their vehicle. Shot on scene at some very gruesome accidents, the raw black and white footage was fully intended to shock and scare.

Denise wasn't going to leave, she was thinking about becoming an undertaker, so why would automobile accident scenes bother her?

The film flickered across the large cream white screen pulled down from over the chalkboard. A State Trooper in a large hat gave the pitch and a final warning.

Three accidents in, Denise took a large gasp. There, stark and focused in center frame, was her Uncle Jeff. He was up to the shoulders through a broken windshield, his sliced face covered with shiny shards of safety glass. The lower jaw was broken back; a piece of the suicide knob it caught while passing over the steering wheel protruded out of the wound. The next picture captured the image from the driver's window looking in. It showed the top half of the wheel bent forward with Jeff's lower chest resting on it. Thick black blood was splattered over the dashboard and front seats. Visible on the passenger's side past Uncle Jeff's broken body was a guitar case flung open by the impact's force. The exposed guitar was not damaged, and even though the film was hard black and white, it appeared as a violent red. Blood from the driver that had landed on the Axe's body and strings was sending up thick curls of smoke.

The camera panned toward the back of the crushed Chevy's interior, then returned to the front seats.

Now closed, the case was so black that Denise could only see its faint outline. Then it vanished completely from her sight.

VI
Rusty Collins

By twenty-seven, he had played every venue possible, large and small. Deep in the Midwest, right after a devastating tornado, Rusty did a three-night fund raiser, fronting a totally different band for each performance. The cash came in hard and fast. He would have been in trouble as a do-gooder for the altruistic act, but the money never made it to the victims.

That day's bad deed ran the donations through Rusty's accountants and into his personal mad-money slush fund.

Rusty pushed the musical envelope, making even the most hard core of players treat him with respect. No one liked him much, but they all wanted to be in his band because, well, it was Hell-hot.

Not only that, his band-mates worked every night getting paid top dollar, when before they were taking fifty cash for a three-hour gig. And it was bands, not band. Rusty played so much it took more than one group to keep up with him.

Every musician that backed Rusty noticed their chops improved tremendously. The few that left quickly fell back to a much lower level. Like everything associated with the

Axe, they, as Johnny Cash once sang, went down, down, down into a burning ring of fire.

VII
Marshall King

Rusty was notorious for bitching out anyone that committed a gaff during a performance. A bass player that flatted a couple of notes and missed a pick up riff was tossed off the bus in the middle of nowhere after he and Rusty had words.

"All I heard from you all night Marshall was fucking clams! It was One, Two, Three, Four, Clam!"

"Come on man, three mistakes. I don't think that's too bad for the second gig."

"I'm fining you five hundred for each one, that's fifteen-hundred bucks."

"Why don't you kiss my black ass, Rusty? You can drop me off at the next stop."

Rusty looked out the window, then back at Marshall. Without another word being said, the tour bus started to slow down. "This is the next stop, motherfucker."

He soon found himself and all of his gear sitting beside a long and lonely road in Big Sky country. It was truly as no-fucking-where as a person could end up. The stranded bass player looked up and down the highway. Now that the tour bus was gone, there wasn't a single light or sign of life in either direction. Still, Marshall was very glad to be off of that bus and out of that band. Musically it was the best band that he had ever played in, but its center was dark.

And that guitar? Rusty Collins practically lived with it. He carried it around all of the time, constantly picking out some riff or strumming a cord pattern. Marshall could not understand Rusty's attraction to the old red guitar. Though no one else noticed, to the bass player the Gibson never seemed to be quite in tune. This wasn't the first time or the worse place that Marshall had found himself alone. Just thirteen short months before he and seven other combat troops were pushing through the thick jungles of Vietnam searching for an elusive, often invisible enemy. They were ambushed by twenty of them and were cut down without mercy. He was the only American soldier that made it out alive that night.

Shipped stateside when his tour of duty was up, the twenty-six-year-old was given a couple of medals and an honorable discharge. With no immediate goals, he retrieved his bass guitar from storage and started practicing. It didn't take long to build the chops back up and find a band. Standing large behind a bunch of stoned lily-white hippies called The Magoos', Marshall King provided the anchor that kept the music from spinning completely off into space.

They traveled to the Midwest to play a three-day festival set up to raise money for some tornado victims.

On the first night, The Magoos' opened for the Rusty Collins Band. It was a night of musical diversity, ranging from the love and beads sound of The Magoos' to the wildfire jamming of Rusty Collins.

Rusty's road manager made an offer to Marshall that he could not refuse. It was a large amount of cash to leave The

Magoos' and join Rusty Collins on the road. The bass player was in need of the money and he was already totally sick of the pot smoking children of love. He accepted the offer.

Luckily it was a warm night in no-where-ville. He carried the large amp and bass guitar to an area off of the side of the road, laid down in a patch of soft grass and dropped into a deep sleep.

No dreams, no worries, no concerns, Marshall was being watched over. Though he was unaware of it, he had just been selected for a very important undertaking. It would take the rest of his life to complete it.

An old pick-up truck chugged by just after sunrise. Marshall, awake for about ten minutes, heard it coming and jumped up from his make-shift bed to stick out his thumb. The old farmer driving did not seem in the least surprised to see a large black man with a bass guitar and an amp hitchhiking along the old country road. He watched in the side mirror as Marshall placed the gear into the rusty bed.

"Thanks for stopping," the bass player said as he climbed into the passenger side. The truck sagged under the additional weight.

"My pleasure." That was the extent of the conversation between them. Twenty-five lonely miles later they came to a crossroads. The driver pulled the rusted-out truck over and pointed to a Greyhound Bus sign planted on the corner. He sat there silently while Marshall unloaded the bass and amp, made a right turn and soon vanished around a bend.

In a few hours a big shiny bus stopped and picked up the now hungry and thirsty musician.

Satan lodged a formal protest. "You had no right to give that man a ride to a bus stop," he complained.

God smiled at his Fallen Angel. "Stop whining, Gadreel, it's your game but it's my rules."

"I will admit though, that was a clever touch dropping him off at a crossroads."

An even bigger smile crossed the Almighty's face. "That's one of the things I still like about you, you get the inside jokes."

The Greyhound carried Marshall King all the way to Seattle, Washington. He quickly found his groove there, working mostly as a hired gun in recording sessions. Firmly established, he would not take any gig further than a day's drive from the city. It was the first place he had ever felt completely comfortable and he was loath to leave it for very long.

When Mr. King laid the bass lines down, the tracks would pop. He had the knack for finding the center of the song and bringing it out. Almost every record from that part of the country that charted had Marshall's low-end signature on it.

The makers of Marshall amplifiers heard Marshall King's sound and hired him to be a spokesman for the line.

Magazine advertising touted, "Marshall prefers Marshalls," showing him standing alongside one of their mainstay JMT45 amp heads. Other ads proclaimed him "The King of Bass." His personal favorite showed a picture of him facing off with John Entwistle, each player holding his main bass with a stack of 4x12 speaker cabinets behind them. The ad read, "Who says Marshall is King?"

The bass player loved the stage in the Eagle's Auditorium and booked his band to play there as much as possible. In a span of just three months during the summer of '68, his band opened for Iron Butterfly, Vanilla Fudge, and Steppenwolf. All three bands played heavy-duty rock-and-roll and were highly impressed at his ability. They tried to get him on the road, but he steadfastly refused. Seattle was home and Marshall intended to stay there.

Life was good and prosperous.

Rusty Collins and his entire band were killed later that year when their tour bus hit a patch of black ice on an Idaho two lane highway. It plunged down a steep embankment into a river that was raging from snow melt off. He was twenty-seven years old.

The Axe was not on the vehicle when it careened off of the road. It had been lifted earlier at a roadside rest stop. A traveling salesman coming out of the restroom peeked into the band's colorfully painted bus out of idle curiosity. There it sat, unguarded. Though he had never stolen a thing in his life, Carl Fischer simply felt compelled to take it.

VIII
Carl Fischer

Satan's guitar sat unplayed in Mr. Fischer's garage in New London, Connecticut for a few months. Existing in ultra-low frequencies, it continued to build its evil authority while waiting for the next chosen one.

Mr. Fischer sold electrical equipment to shipbuilders for a large east coast manufacturer. He was on the road a lot, and being downright afraid of flying, drove to all of his sales meetings. He would often take his wife, Sharon, along and take advantage of the expense paid trips. About a year earlier she had stopped going, saying that she was tired of the travel. Carl suspected Sharon was having an affair with their next-door neighbor.

On the way back from a sales and equipment demonstration seminar in Bremerton, Washington, the call of nature caused him to pull over at a rest stop in Idaho. While there he peeked into a tour bus, saw a guitar case, and on sudden impulse stole it. Feeling both guilty and liberated for committing the crime, Carl started thinking about all of the other dishonest things he had never done. Something tugged at him and convinced him that maybe he was being too good goody. Where had it gotten him? Nowhere really.

That night at a hotel bar, for the first time, he picked up a hooker. Mr. Fischer's personal behavior dam was starting to crack.

He soon discovered Sharon was indeed screwing the neighbor, and drinking wine to heavy excess as well. It was time to take some action. Divorce was out of the question. Carl did not want that bitch to get any of his hard-earned money, or the way too expensive house that she loved so much. He came up with a plan that would rid him of both problems. All that he needed was a willing helper and a decent alibi.

Carl Fischer had the perfect payment for this dirty deed available. It was sitting in his garage in a double-black case.

IX
Scorpion

She left her last port of call in Rota, Spain, on a mission to monitor Soviet Naval activity near the Azores Islands. A few days after patrolling on station, the nuclear-powered Skipjack class submarine turned west toward the United States and home. On May 21st, 1968, communications with the USS Scorpion SSN 589 were lost. A major malfunction sent her with two nuclear torpedoes below crush depth and scattered the remains across the sandy ocean bottom ten-thousand feet below the North Atlantic's surface.

X
Spike

"What do you want for it, Mr. Fischer?" Spike's eyes were wide with anticipation at the thought of owning the guitar beautifully nestled in the case on the table before him. "It's the most perfect thing I've ever seen."

"You can't just buy this guitar my friend, you have to earn it."

"What do you need me to do? I'll do anything you want."

"Really? Anything?"

"I said anything and that's what I mean, anything!"

Carl Fischer could tell by the look on Spike's face that he was telling the truth. "Well, I have a house that is costing me way more than it's worth. If it happened to catch on fire while I was out of town, the insurance money would set me right."

"That's it. That's what you want?"

"It has to look like an accident so no one will be suspicious."

"Hell's bells, I'm an Electrician's Mate on a nuclear-powered submarine, I should be able to figure something out."

"Are you going to sea anytime soon?"

"As a matter of fact, we're leaving on extended patrol next week." Spike did not care that he was telling this unknown man highly secret information. He could only see himself playing that guitar.

"Then you are definitely the right guy. It would be better if you are not around after the fire. Pull it off this weekend while I'm in New York and the guitar is yours."

"Can I take it with me now?"

"Not a chance, I'll hang onto it until you've finished the job."

Spike stood across the street by an alley entrance and watched as the blaze grew until it began to show through a large bay window. That was way too fucking easy, he thought.

He frayed an old lamp cord lying close to a rug by sliding it back and forth under his shoe sole until the insulation was worn through. Then he sprinkled a very small amount of pure alcohol around to ensure the spark would ignite the fringe. It was submarine cleaning alcohol and was so pure that it would leave no residue to garner suspicion.

Bang! One perfect arson. The entire front of the house was quickly engulfed. In the distance and closing fast, the firetruck sirens screamed as they made their approach.

He turned and walked down the alleyway fantasizing that he was already playing that incredible guitar. Behind him another high pitch cut through all of the other commotion. It was in the same key as the music in Spike's head, only it was a human voice and sang of massive pain.

Layered over the imagined music, it became an exciting solo.

Turning back, he saw a figure covered with flames run out of the house and across the yard.

It was frantically waving its arms and making the most agonizing sounds he had ever heard. He was not in the least bothered.

The following Tuesday Carl Fischer and Spike met again. The brand-new widower brought the guitar along to pay off his debt.

Spike eyed it and smiled; the treasure was almost his.

"You didn't tell me your wife was going to be home, Fischer. Arson is bad enough, but I damn sure don't want to be implicated in a murder!"

"Don't worry, you won't. The preliminary report says that it was caused by a worn lamp cord. Sharon was passed out as usual and didn't wake up in time. Her death is being called accidental. I didn't carry any life insurance on her, so with an airtight alibi and no obvious motive, the investigation should end. You, my friend, did an excellent job."

"Were you trying to get rid of the house or the wife?"

"Both. The house was a money pit and the wife couldn't stay away from the booze or the next-door neighbor. Now I'm rid of two pains-in-the-ass. I thought if you knew someone was in there you might not do it."

Spike thought about the case resting on the seat between them, its blackness began to pull him in.

Showing his impatience, he snarled. "I would have burned up your whole fucking family and the dog too. Now, give me my guitar!"

Taken aback by the vehement answer, Mr. Fischer realized how badly he wanted to get rid of that guitar and away from the angry sailor. "Take it, it's yours. Hopefully you'll have better luck with it than I have. I tried to play the damn thing once and couldn't even get it in tune." He handed the case over to Spike. The sailor took it knowing that keeping it in tune would not be a problem at all.

Taking the Axe to sea on the boat wasn't a problem either, and since he was already qualified, he had plenty of time to practice. Making sure he had his hands on its silky neck at 2400 hours was a bit tricky because of the six-hour watch rotation, but so far Spike had managed to pull it off.

XI
The Scorpion Departs
But Never Returns

The min-overhaul completed, Scorpion left Norfolk and headed east, eventually docking in Rota, Spain. On the trip over she was plagued with numerous equipment failures.

None were big enough to force her to turn around, but they did cause the enlisted crew to bitch about the job done during her stay in the shipyard. They started calling her the USS Scrap Iron.

Spike was unconcerned about any of it, he only cared when a problem took him away from playing the Axe. Often when he was practicing on the mess deck or in the torpedo room, the off-watch sailors would gather around to listen. They tried to stump him with song requests, everything from the hits of the day to obscure stuff, even symphonies. Spike would laugh and pick out the melodies without fail.

"So, Willie, what are you gonna do when we finally hit port?"

"Me? Chubby, my friend, I'll tell you what I'm gonna do. I'm going to dance, prance, and romance. Then, I'm going to fuck, suck, and run amok."

The Ensign, standing his first training watch, spoke sharply. "Sounds like you've got a busy schedule planned there, sailor. Now stop screwing around and pay attention to the panel!"

"Yes Sir! Just trying to keep up the moral here in Maneuvering, Sir."

The 1st Class Electricians Mate picked up a clipboard and began to take the hourly logs, noting the values shown on the various gauges and dials covering the control panel. Fucking newbies, he thought, always sweating the small shit. I qualified two fucking boats while this guy was still pissing in his diapers.

On the mess deck MM2 Baxter and IC1 Clarke were deeply involved in a game of chess. The ship's medic, a first-class Petty Officer, came out of the very small medical office. Baxter noticed him and said, "Hey Doc, attack your artichoke."

To which the Doc replied, "Banging your beef stick." The sailors both laughed and then Doc headed aft to collect the Nucs' dosimeters and check radiation exposure.

"What was that all about?" Clarke asked.

"Doc and I do it on every run. We start at the top of the alphabet and try to come up with different ways to say jacking off. The next time I see him I'll have to have something that starts with C. I'm thinking choking your chicken or creaming your carrot."

"Baxter, you are one crude fucking dude."

"Thank you, Clarke. By the way, checkmate."

"Damn it! Do you want to go again?"

"Sure, if you don't mind losing again."

The Engineering Watch Supervisor stuck his head into the small room and reported that everything was normal in the Engineering Spaces. Catching the Electrical Operator's eye he asked, "Hey Willie, have you heard Spike playing that new guitar of his? Man has he got the heat! He makes it sing even without an amplifier."

"Something about that guitar gives me the creeps," Willie answered. "He practically lives with the damn thing when he's off duty. The other guys store their axes in the torpedo room, but Spike keeps his strapped into the top of his rack. That leaves him with about three inches above his face when he sleeps."

"Maybe he's fucking it," Chubby chimed in.

Everyone in Maneuvering laughed except the Ensign.

"Knock it off!"

Right then all Hell began to calmly break loose.

Over the 1MC a steady voice commanded. "This is the Captain speaking. This is not a drill. Man battle stations. Rig ship for reduced electrical. Rig ship for ultra-silence. Shift propulsion to the Electric Propulsion Motor."

In the Sonar shack the Scorpion's Skipper, Lieutenant Commander Francis Slattery, placed the microphone back into its overhead holder.

He and the two operators were closely watching a green blip on the passive sonar screen. The blip was moving toward them at a steady pace.

The Captain spoke, his voice and demeanor hiding the sudden concern he felt, "I'm heading for Control, keep me informed on our friend's movements. Let me know who it is as soon as you figure it out." With that he quickly left to take the Conn. Whomever this was, and he had his suspicions, they were about to find out what it was to deal first-hand with a United State's nuclear-powered submarine.

"This is the Captain, I have the Conn. Chief, I believe our friend out there is getting into position to shoot at us. I want MK14 war shot loaded into all tubes, electronic counter-measures prepared, and a constant update for firing solutions on the contact."

"Aye, aye, sir." A few minutes later he reported, "Sir, battle-stations are manned, torpedoes are loaded, and we are rigged for ultra-silence. We are also ready to answer all bells on the Electric Propulsion Motor."

"Aye, Chief, send a well done to the crew for getting us battle ready so quick. Keep those solutions coming."

"What are you doing there, Carlson?" the Sonar Officer asked.

"Sir, I'm wiping the woman's names off of the seamounts."

When he was on watch, Petty Officer Carlson would use a dry marker to label any seamounts located in the area with the names of females that he had slept with. "I don't want the Captain to get pissed at me."

"He won't say a word, this is some real shit we're in right now and the only thing the Old Man cares about is that we all do our jobs and not fuck up."

Carlson continued cleaning the names off of the charts. "Just the same, sir, I'm not taking any chances."

"Leave Jenny up there, that's my ex-wife's name and that seamount does look a lot like her spread. Say, Carlson, you didn't bang my ex-old lady, did you?"

"I don't ask them their last names, sir, so I'm not sure."

"Well, everybody else has, so don't worry about it."

Carlson, long time qualified on both pig and nuclear boats, was not in the least afraid of junior officers. "Sir, the next time you see her you should ask her. I may not remember her, but she will damn sure remember me." A few seconds later, the Petty Officer spoke again. He was now very serious. "Sir, the contact is slowing and is turning directly toward us. Her sound signature is the same as the Russian sub we were tailing last week."

"Very well, Carlson." The Sonar Officer passed the word to the Captain, then settled back to watching the ominous blip.

He had a pretty good idea what was going to happen next.

The Scorpion had been ordered to slip in and monitor some Russian Fleet maneuvers around the Azores. The Captain thought they had accomplished the mission undetected, but the situation now seemed to suggest differently.

They had in fact succeeded, the Russians never had a clue that the American submarine was anywhere near them. Unknown to the crew of the USS Scorpion, a Chief Petty Officer by the name of John Walker Jr. betrayed them. A long-time traitor with complete access to sensitive Naval communications, he sold their mission and expected route to the enemy. The submarine engaging them was waiting on Scorpion's return course. She was sent by the Politburo to extract revenge for the Soviet boat, K-129 hull number 722. The Russian sub had been sunk by the Americans off of the Hawaiian Islands the previous March.

"Control, Sonar, the contact has slowed. It's a Ruskie fast attack and she's flooding her forward tubes."

"Sonar, Conn, aye. What is her bearing, depth, and distance?"

"Starboard bearing, forty-eight degrees at one-hundred and fifty feet.

She's six thousand yards out and closing at two knots."

He spoke to the sailor standing next to him. "Chief, how the hell did she get so close?"

"Don't know Sir, we usually hear these bastards well before ten miles."

A single ping came from the Russian's active sonar.

"Control, Sonar, there's a torpedo in the water!"

"Helm! Ten degree down bubble. All ahead full. Take her to four-hundred feet."

A few moments later, the entire crew heard the torpedo's propeller blades cutting through the water above. It emitted a high-pitched whine, a very thin and delicate sound for such a destructive device. "That was fucking close! Helm, maintain four-hundred feet. Let's stay well below the thermal-clime, do a tight circle and flank this bitch. When we get the opportunity, we are going to send her to the bottom." All of the men stationed in the Conn nodded with approval.

Captain Slattery drew a deep breath then ordered, "Make turns for two knots. Helm, fight full rudder."

"Aye, aye, sir!" The crew of the Scorpion was ready to kick some Russian ass.

Even though the enemy was able to surprise them and take the first shot, the near miss meant they were still in the game and a very formidable foe.

"Pass the word over the sound-powered phones, she's gonna come down here looking for us. I want this boat quiet, no fucking noise by anyone for any reason. Got it?"

The phone-talker passed along the Captain's orders as the fire control party eagerly searched for a targeting solution.

Spike was beginning to get nervous. It was rapidly approaching midnight and his battle-station was in the main compartment as a phone-talker. If they remained in this condition for much longer, he would not be able to get to his rack and his hands on the Axe. He knew in the very core of his soul that if he was not playing it at the required time, all was lost. Even if he could get a watch relief, being rigged for silence would prevent him from striking a single note.

In the Sonar shack, the petty officer monitoring the stack heard the faint sound of music. As it grew louder in his head phones, he could clearly hear a blistering guitar riff being played over and over.

Da-da-daa-daah-da-daa-daah-da-daa-daah-da-daa daa.

Da-da-daa-daah-da-daa-daah-da-daa-daah-dadaa daa.

Carlson was a guitar player himself and could tell it was an A note, switching to a G, then an F, then back to the G. It was hypnotic.

Eight years later that riff would fill the FM radio air waves.

The clock on the bulkhead was only a few minutes from both hands pointing straight up. Sweat started to pour from every inch of Spike's body, accompanied by uncontrolled shaking. The compartment roving watch noticed and incorrectly assumed that Spike was reacting to the enemy attack. "Take it easy guy, the Old Man will pull us out of this."

"Fuck you, Kroger!" The clock now read dead on twenty-four hundred hours. Spike yanked off his headphones and started choking the watch-stander. In the overhead of Spike's rack, the Axe began to heat up, sending thick curls of white smoke into the bunk room. Spike's cursing voice and the loud struggle could be clearly heard on the Conn. At the same time, the word was being passed over the sound-powered phone system: "Fire in the twenty-two-man bunk room!"

Another single ping of active sonar penetrated the boat's hull, followed closely by the rush of multiple torpedoes.

"Emergency blow! Emergency blow!" Slattery bellowed. Water belched from the vents starting the Scorpion rushing rapidly toward the surface. The brace of torpedoes fired by the Russian boat passed harmlessly beneath them.

At two hundred fifty feet and rising, the unmistakable sound of flooding roared through the forward section. Spike, now completely out of his mind, used his knowledge of the boat's systems to open the Trash Disposal Unit's one-and-a-half-inch pipe to sea. The sudden weight of the incoming water overwhelmed the emergency blow and sent the now doomed submarine and crew down to be crushed in the ocean's unmerciful depths.

The USS Scorpion, SSN 589, broke apart and settled on the bottom. She became the second US submarine bearing that name to go on Eternal Patrol.

Sea water rushed into what was left of the twenty-two-man bunk room and covered the case tucked in Spike's rack. It burst into hot white flames, searing the cords that held it in place, allowing it to be swept away by invisible currents.

It was time to find a new player.

XII
Looking for A Home

A couple of weeks later a fishing trawler out of Gloucester, casting her nets in Georges Bank for Cod, caught an unusually large shark. The crew of the Minnow killed and cut it open to find out what it had been eating. They had seen all kinds of weird stuff fall out of a shark's belly before, but never a guitar case. When the goo-covered case was opened, they were even more surprised to see that it was completely dry inside, and the blood-red guitar was in perfect tune. Shortly after, the sailor that strummed it got his hands chopped cleanly off by a snapped winch cable. The unfortunate fisherman was transferred to the trawler Whitby Rose. Her holds were full and she was on her way back to port.

During the rest of her trip, the Minnow hauled Cod in faster than ever, sending them home early with a record catch.

The first day in port, the Minnow's Captain, a man that liked to drink Jack Daniel's whiskey and play poker, made some bad decisions at the table. Lady Luck turned her back and he lost the Axe to a fat cigar smoker.

The cigar smoker bluffed the Captain out with a pair of deuces.

The cursed guitar left the poker game with the cigar smoker. He often joked that when it came to musical ability, he could only play the radio. There was one member of the family that could play though, and that was his beloved granddaughter, Serriana. She had shown natural talent from the tender age of five when she started picking out popular melodies on the piano.

XIII
Serriana

Serriana was a honey-blond beauty with a voice as pure and smooth as virgin silk. A deep love for country music ran through her, the simple song structure and clever turn of phrase gave her unbounded pleasure. Her romance with the Axe lasted a long time. It was intense and eventually tragic.

Serriana's gambling grandfather died in late June of 1967. Her mother spent the week in Boston with him before he passed. He told her that a guitar he recently won in a poker game was to be given to his struggling musician granddaughter, Serriana. She did just that on the day of the funeral.

As Serriana ran her hands over the incredible instrument, she wondered how anybody would take a chance losing it in a card game. It made no difference, now it belonged to her! She felt very powerful and in control.

A back-up band fell quickly into place. The ramp up of her career was phenomenal.

Serriana and her band were on their first official tour. They were booked to play a week's worth of shows the month of August in Chicago. By coincidence it was during the '68 National Democratic Convention. While there, she met the nationally acclaimed folksinger Phil Ochs. He was protesting the military-industrial complex, she was making music and money.

Serriana really liked Phil's song *I Ain't Marching Anymore*. She didn't tell Phil, but she was for the war. Any war, not just Vietnam. The pictures of American soldiers returning home in body bags gave her secret pleasure.

When she heard that he was in Chicago to support the movement, she made a point to seek him out. They spent an afternoon in a cheap motel room, smoking pot, trading songs, and having sex.

Phil was enchanted by her beautiful guitar.

For some reason while he was playing it, he started to think about the nuclear submarine that had went down with all hands the previous May. Singing about lost submarines wasn't new to Phil, he had written a song about the USS Thresher SSN 593 after she sunk during initial sea trials in April of 1963.

The very next time he sat down at a piano, he came up with a song about the sinking of the Scorpion. Not too long after he laid his hands on Serriana's wicked Axe, Phil Ochs became a hard core revolutionary. He went from just singing protest songs to being a front-line participant. His strong involvement with the counterculture and populist movement got him noticed and followed by the FBI. A righteous paranoia set in and he turned into an alcoholic with a bipolar personality. He tried to become Elvis Presley and failed. Miserably, He tried to become Che Guevara and failed. Miserably. He tried to kill off Phil Ochs by becoming the hammer carrying John Butler Train. Again, he failed. Miserably. In 1976, Phil gave up and hanged himself. He finally succeeded and silenced all of the conflicting voices in his head.

A tune penned by Serriana's lover, *You Hit My Heart Like a Train*, went straight up the charts.

One night he got hit by a locomotive while walking on the railroad tracks, as drunk as he could possibly be. The macabre accident fueled the song's rocket launch to the top.

The second chart topper, *You Can't Spell Hell Without He*, told of a young woman's relationship with an abusive husband. It had a happy ending. She shot him to death when he started slapping her around for spilling a beer.

At the beginning of each show Serriana would introduce The Demimondaines, three female backup singers dressed in sexy black gowns. She called them her accessories. Much more than eye-candy, they danced in haunting synchronization using tightly choreographed moves. They sang like angels. The drummers, bass players, or lead players were never mentioned, or even acknowledged during a performance. There was good cause for this, the male members of the band never lasted long. Serriana used them like toothpicks. She saw no reason to waste her time trying to remember all of their names. A couple of different times a bass player was replaced during a show. On one occasion the drummer was actually changed in the middle of a song. The audience never noticed.

Fatigue, brought on by excessive amounts of drugs, alcohol, and sex, was the main reason no man ever made it through more than one tour or recording project. Serriana burned through them. They were nothing more than cord wood to power her amazing music machine.

Country music would never be the same after Serriana put her brand on it. She racked up hit after hit and sold out every venue. Always in control, she had only one really bad moment. That was during a Seattle show in May of '74. For some reason the Axe would not stay in tune. She turned down the volume level and tried to fake it, but the fans noticed a huge drop from her usual high energy level.

The country star exited the stage and did not go back out for an encore. Serriana called her manager from a backstage phone. "Never book this fucking city again!" she shouted at him. "In fact, cancel any show we have in the whole fucking state of Washington!"

"But, Serriana, why? We've got two more gigs set up for this tour, including the second tomorrow night there in Seattle. They're both sold out."

"Cancel them!"

"You're going to disappoint a lot of fans and lose a lot of cash."

"I don't give a fuck! If you want to keep your job, the next time I talk to you, those shows had better be goddamned canceled!"

Shaken by the anger in her voice, he agreed to pull the plug on the two shows and hung up.

It was too late, a primal force had been awakened from a very deep sleep. It was off to a long slow start, but the war between Good and Evil was now being engaged on a new front. This battle was so important that if Good lost, it might well be the end of Good. At the same time that Serriana's guitar was acting up, Marshall King was experiencing difficulties as well. He was unable to find the groove or concentrate. Hell, he couldn't even keep his bass in tune.

The studio tech poured over the heavy Fender Jazz Master, but could not find a reason for the problem. It played and sounded perfect to him.

While making one last attempt to get the strings in tune, a sudden vision punched into Marshall's plane of consciousness. The Axe, that Gibson ES-335 once owned by Rusty Collins, was nearby.

He had been surprised when Serriana turned up with famous hollow-body. Marshall assumed it was lost when Rusty's bus crashed into that river in Idaho. She was in town tonight, fronting her band with it.

He was beginning to understand what was going on, and that it could eventually consume him. Marshall now realized that his future was set. He was destined for a confrontation with the Axe, up front and personal. Fuck! Life was going so good.

Marshall apologized to the artist and ended the session.

Back in her dressing room Serriana was twisting on the Axe's pegs trying to get it into tune. It simply would not co-operate. There was no tone, the strings were dead and covered with sweat and corrosion. For the first time since her grandfather left her the guitar. Serriana felt unsettled and unsure.

She lovingly laid the faded and scratched Axe back into the now dull black case. She hoped that when she picked it up at midnight to play that it would become restored.

The one thing she did know, she had to get the hell out of Seattle! Something in this city was interfering with the Axe's power.

There were some friends in a Portland suburb that would put her up, no questions asked.

Serriana called in the new head roadie, "Tell the band I'm leaving for Oregon. I'll meet up with them next week in Portland for our concert there."

"Don't we have another show here tomorrow night?"

"No, it's canceled. Call a limo service and make arrangements for a car to pick me up and drive me down to Beaverton."

"You don't want to fly?"

"Why do you care how I fucking get there? Call the limo, tell them to be here in ten minutes!"

The roadie couldn't believe that she was talking to him like that. Just yesterday they had made passionate love in his hotel room. Serriana had showed up after the sound check with a coke filled tin and a bottle of wine to welcome him to his job with the band. It was an evening of drugs and wild sex. She left him a few minutes before midnight, rushing out of the room on what appeared to be blackened silk wings.

Ten minutes later, Serriana got into the limo with no luggage other than the faded black Gibson case. The roadie held the door open for her and wished her a safe ride. She looked back at him and made a snap decision.

"Come on, I want you to ride down with me."

"I'm not packed or ready."

"Don't worry, anything you need we can pick up. Get in." Serriana was thinking that in a few hours when she would have to be playing the Axe, she might need a sacrifice to help return it to its former glory.

The head roadie knew better than to argue and climbed into the plush back seat beside her. She pushed the intercom button and ordered the driver. "Let's go." As the limo sped south from Seattle on Interstate 5, the Axe's case, lying on the seat opposite of Serriana and the roadie, began to get blacker.

Back on Whidbey Island, the tuning problem with Marshall King's bass guitar cleared up.

They reached Olympia in a little over an hour.

Serriana instructed the driver to get off of the interstate. He was to head west and pick up the Pacific highway southbound. In Astoria they made a stop at a gas station. Right before they left, she got out of the back and moved to the front passenger seat. The roadie, all buzzed up on pot and cocaine, didn't seem to notice her absence. The limo driver was used to movie and rock stars doing unusual things, so he didn't object. This was one sexy woman and he was delighted to have her sitting in the seat beside him. She slipped close and began to rub the back of her hand on his leg. "I've got a favor to ask of you."

"What's that?"

"I can't think of the name of it, but there is a state park by Arch Cape that I want to stop at."

"You're thinking of Oswald West State Park."

"That sounds right."

"We'll pass by it at eleven-thirty or so. It's going to be way too dark to see anything or go onto any of the trails."

"That's okay, for what I need to do the darkness is good. I'll make it well worth your while." With that she leaned against him and kissed his ear.

He smiled. "Anything to keep the customer happy." The roadie snorted another line, passed out and fell forward onto the opposite seat. A small amount of blood seeped from his cocaine battered nose and dripped onto the guitar case. A bright but cold light flared off of it. Inside, the Axe responded and began to vibrate.

The flash startled the driver. "What was that!?" Serriana lifted her head from his lap and answered. "Nothing, don't worry about it." She looked around then asked, "How long to the state park?"

"About fifteen minutes. Do you really want to stop there?"

"Yes, it's very important that we do. By the way, most of the limo drivers I know carry a gun. How about you?"

"I wouldn't leave home without it, I drive a lot of important people around and I want to be able to protect them if I should need to."

"Where is it?"

The driver reached down and pulled it from a holster attached to the steering column. It was a Smith and Wesson .38 five shot revolver, "Right here where I can grab it fast."

"Perfect. Pull over as soon as you see one of the park trails." Serriana then put her face back into his lap. Twenty minutes later he spotted a sign that marked a hiking trial on the right-hand side of the road. He slowed, pulled the limo as far off of the pavement as he could and stopped.

Serriana jumped out and retrieved the guitar case from the back seat. She shook the roadie by his shoulder and told him, "Get up, come on we're going to take a walk."

Above the empty highway a billion stars filled the sky. The edge of the forest looked like a wall, solid and impenetrable. The limo driver slipped the .38 into his coat pocket and followed the other two toward the path. When he stepped over the thick black line into the deep woods he had to stop and let his eyes adjust to the darkness. It took about forty-five seconds before he could see Serriana and the roadie. She seemed to be having no problem finding her way along the trail.

A short distance in the rest of the world disappeared. They could neither see nor hear traffic from the road behind them, or the ocean's waves crashing against the steep cliffs ahead. Serriana continued another hundred feet or so then placed the case on a fallen tree trunk. She pulled out the Axe and began to play, relieved that it was back in tune and shining a wicked red again. The confused roadie weakly resisted when she demanded that he kneel down. A couple of pushes from the driver put him on his knees in front of Serriana looking up at her. She continued to play. Each note and riff burned into his addled brain. She looked at the driver with eyes bright from an internal light. "You know what to do."

Right at the stroke of midnight he placed the revolver to the back of the drugged-up roadie's head and joyfully squeezed the trigger. Blood and brain matter splattered all over the guitar, the strings began to smoke. The power was back!

Back on Whidbey Island, the lights in Marshall's studio flickered twice, then went completely off.

XIV
Buck Dharma and
Blue Oyster Cult

"What a great job, Serriana! This is going to be your best album yet. I cannot believe how great these songs are! With all of your touring, when do you ever find the time to write?"

The beautiful country star and her engineer were up on the famous studio's flat roof. There were wooden planting boxes and pots scattered about. Green leafy stuff poked out of the boxes, the pots contained various types of small tomatoes. The bright greens, reds and yellows contrasted sharply against the roof's black and gravel pitch.

"Thank you, Shelley," she responded. "I knocked all of them off except *Death of a Roadie* in hotel rooms and on tour buses."

Standing just behind the short wall that encompassed the top, she gazed over 10th Avenue and West 51st Street, towards the heart of Hell's Kitchen. Turning to face southeast, she could see the Empire State Building lording over Midtown.

"Where did you write that one?" he continued.

"In Oregon last year while I was staying with some friends. It's the first one that I wrote for the project."

"Well, I have to say that one is my favorite even though it's more folk than country. It sounds like something Phil Ochs might have written."

"Wow! You sure do know your music, Shelly. I hung out with Phil in Chicago in '68 and I freely admit that it was heavily influenced by his style."

"What a shame he killed himself, it must have been terrible for his sister to find him hanging like that." Shelley had turned away. He did not see Serriana's sarcastic little smile. "Yes, a real shame. Poor Phil was just too sensitive for this world."

The house engineer shook his head sadly then said, "Let's go back to the control room and listen to the final mixes one more time before the next band loads in."

"Okay by me, who've you got booked?"

"Blue Oyster Cult."

"Oh. I really like that live album they cut last year. Too bad I have to fly to Houston and can't stick around to meet them. Are you going to be their engineer?"

"Yes, I am, and so is Roy. He's working with a local band for a few days then taking over when I go on vacation."

"Hey," Buck asked the engineer. "Whose guitar is this? I know it's not one of ours."

Busy zeroing the recording console, Shelly Yakus took a look over his shoulder into the hallway that cut behind the control room. His faced registered surprise. "Oh shit! That belongs to Serriana. She just left a few hours ago. I can't fucking believe it's still here! I worked on the whole project and she always kept it with her. I'd better call her or her manager right away!"

One of the unpaid assistants spoke up. "They're both on a plane to Houston. A limo took them straight to the airport from here."

"You let her leave without her guitar?"

"Don't blame me Shelly," the assistant shrugged, "I can't keep up with everything. Besides, isn't that her manager's job?"

"Yeah, you're right. Find a way to get it to her double fucking fast though."

"You got it Shelly, double fucking fast is my normal speed around here."

"Can I see it? It belonged to Rusty Collins, right?"

"Yes, it did, Buck. Serriana told me that her grandpa won it in a poker game." The engineer then shook his head no. "She doesn't let anyone touch that guitar, not even a tech. I still can't believe that she left it behind."

"I'm not gonna play it, I just want to see it up close."

Shelly hesitated. "Alright, just a peek." Out in the sound booth, a couple of the band members started warming up on their instruments for the guide tracks to Don't Fear the Reaper.

A while later, the band gathered in the control room to listen to the tape playback.

"How about that, Shelly! One take on the whole rhythm section and solo tracks!" Buck and the band where ecstatic, the guitars swirled around in the mix like hypnotic snakes.

"Listen to me," Shelly said. "I still don't think it was a very good idea to play Serriana's guitar." Shelly loved the sound, but was plainly uncomfortable with Buck's decision to use the instrument without her permission. "Oh, hell yes, it was Shelly! It definitely fucking was! Didn't you just hear that riff and solo? Anyway, how's Serriana ever gonna know if nobody tells her?"

"I have a feeling she'll know."

The second hand on the studio reception area's clock swept past eleven o'clock as Buck stepped into the hallway and reluctantly returned the incredible guitar to its coffin-like case. He hoped Serriana wouldn't be too pissed about him using it, but he knew that if she found out, she would be. Buck had heard a few rumors about her, none of them good.

How strange that right after he ripped off that righteous take, the guitar would no longer stay in tune. It had also become very cold to the touch.

The guitar dropped easily back into the perfect silk lined cutout. Buck ran his finger over the Axe one last time. Bright, cold white light blasted across his face. A huge swarm of bats filled his vision, so many that he thought it must be all of them in the world. In the distance he could hear an airplane.

The impression lasted a few seconds before Buck snapped back into reality.

Through the opened door to the control room Buck heard the producer say to the rhythm guitarist, "Eric, I think we need to add a cowbell to accent the downbeat."

XV
Souls on Fire

Serriana was totally happy. She sat alone in the front of the Gulfstream's passenger cabin looking out a small window at the lights on the tarmac. Her back-up singers, the Demimondaines, were curled up together on a large sofa and already fast asleep. They were worn out. The recording sessions had been extensive and tiring. And, while they were waiting in the limo to leave for the airport, Serriana introduced them to a young boy named Graham. He was looking for autographs.

He got far more than autographs.

Her manager was also sleeping, sprawled across one of the two single beds at the rear of the cabin.

The rest of the band was on the tour bus with the gear. They were passing by the New York City limit sign on their way to Houston. A slight detour and a stop in Ohio was planned. They needed to pick up a new lead guitar player. The one they used in the studio had burned himself to death a few days earlier while freebasing cocaine in his hotel room with a prostitute.

Houston was one of Serriana's favorite cities. It had anything and everything she wanted. The great sessions and the anticipation of a few days off had her in a very good mood. On the following Friday she and the backup singers were going to meet up with the band and start the next tour. Until then it was party time!

As soon as the plane lifted off, she fired up a joint and relaxed back into the seat watching the lights on the ground grow smaller and smaller before the cloud ceiling at twelve thousand feet swallowed them up. The plane proceeded to forty-one thousand feet, well above commercial traffic, and leveled off. The pilot and co-pilot settled in for a routine flight.

Life was really good until right before midnight.

At a quarter-to-twelve Serriana went to the back of the plane's cabin to retrieve the Axe. When she pulled the curtain back on the storage space area, she saw that it was not there.

Panic set in! She quickly roused the manager from his deep sleep. "Where is my Axe!?" She screamed into his ear.

The manager, startled and groggy, responded. "The last time I saw it, it was sitting in the hallway by the control room at the studio. I thought you grabbed it." In the cockpit the pilot suddenly noticed a large mass on the plane's radar screen. At first he thought it was another plane on a direct course toward them. The copilot saw it a second later. "What is that?" The pilot shoved the yoke hard down to avoid a collision, but the mass dropped as well and stayed in front of them. Within seconds they could see what the thick mass was not a solid object, it was a swarm of vampire bats.

"What the fuck?" The pilot exclaimed. "Bats never fly above ten-thousand feet!"

"The Hell they don't!" yelled the freaked-out co-pilot.

Sharp. staccato noises began to permeate the plane, pounding on the hull like they were inside a large drum kit being played by the Devil himself.

The co-pilot barely had time to send out a May Day before the engines, clogged with the bodies of ingested bats, shut down.

The Gulfstream glided for a short while, then fell out of the sky and smashed onto the tranquil Texas landscape below. Everybody on board was killed instantly.

The ultra-black case was still sitting in the New York recording studio hallway. The Axe had just been used by Blue Oyster Cult to record one of the most famous riffs in modern rock and roll. Once again it took on a dingy and shabby look. Inside, the guitar went into cold hibernation. No fanfare, no ceremony, no passage of rite. It was time to move on.

In Seattle, as Serriana's ill-fated flight rapidly approached the dark mass, Marshall King woke from an uneasy sleep. The room was humming loudly with what sounded like airplane engines. Smooth and steady at first, they began to stutter, then the noise level increased as they started to strain. Cutting with a sharp edge, complete silence then filled the bedroom.

A moment later he heard the repeated words,

Mayday! Mayday! A piercing dark laughter began to swell out of the total quiet. It got so loud that Marshall had to cover his ears with his palms to protect the delicate membranes from damage. He swore he could smell jet fuel and burning flesh.

Marshall broke into a cold sweat that soaked and stained his bedding.

Serriana's last creation, *Souls on Fire*, was released three months after the plane crash. It was by far and large the best-selling of her career. *Death of a Roadie* premiered as a single thirty days before the full album was released, it stayed on the charts for years. Six years, six months, and six hours after it's early debut, there was a sharp rise in deaths by self-inflicted gunshot. No single profile covered all of the victims. They were troubled youths, middle-class mothers, uncles, grandfathers; a whole mix of different types. The other one thing that the suicides had in common, besides the use of a .38 revolver, was that *Death of a Roadie* was playing on repeat at each scene.

XVI
Graham Graves

The next recipient to bargain his soul away was a father-less seventeen-year-old New York City boy. Born in Hell's Kitchen, he was skinny, mean, and fiercely driven. Because he could convincingly act charming and be polite for short periods of time, he was able to easily talk people into doing things for him.

His life was an absolute perfect model of destruction. Everything and everyone he touched ended up fucked over or fucked-up. Usually both. It was as natural as thunder and lightning or volcanoes and earthquakes. Christened Graham Graves, he was simply unable to get along with others for very long. Graham struck out on his own early, leaving home and high school two months and one credit short of graduation. The typing teacher wouldn't pass him because he had skipped thirty-three of the forty-four required days of class attendance. It was all so boring.

He killed the typing teacher's cat, then left its body under the passenger side back tire of her car. She felt the bump when she backed up, and broke into hysterical tears when she got out and saw her pet smashed into the driveway.

Celebrating his seventeenth time around the sun had been a blast.

He killed his first guy with a borrowed pistol that day. The thing was a total piece of shit. If Graham had aimed it properly, he would have missed the target completely. Unfortunately for the victim, Graham was shooting wildly and hit the poor bastard twice. It turned out to be just pure bad luck to be on the barrel side of that gun.

Then came the serious shit.

Located south and a little east of where Graham lived sat the history making recording studio, The Record Plant. Graham liked to hang out on West 44th Street and watch for rock stars and get their autographs.

He would always ask a roadie or limo driver to snap a picture of them signing with him in it. Graham may have been lacking a degree in public education, but he no dummy. Pictures were proof and he knew they would make his collection extremely valuable someday. Each time, he would respectfully approach and introduce himself, then politely ask for an autograph. His collection of famous people's pictures and signatures was impressive.

He couldn't believe his luck! Coming out the main door with one of her minions in tow was none other than the biggest country star of the day, Serriana!

My God! She was even hotter live than she was on the posters and album covers. Oh yeah!

His heart ticked up several beats. With pad and pen in hand he walked straight to her. "Hello Serriana, my name is Graham Graves. May I please have your autograph?"

"How could I not say yes to such a polite young man?" She repeated his name as she signed the pad, then looked him over. "I like your eyes Mr. Graves.

How old are you?"

"Seventeen last March."

"Listen, would you like the Demimondaines to give you their autographs as well?"

"That would be something!"

"They're in the back of the limo, come across the street with me and I will introduce you." Then, a coy question, "I hope you're not in a hurry to be someplace?"

Graham caught on. "No hurry at all," he replied.

Serriana, very eager to share her new friend with her old friends, did not realize that the Axe was no longer in her possession.

It was cooling its heels in a studio hallway, waiting to get the Master's first riff and solo recorded.

Getting the back-up singers autographs was the most satisfying thing Graham had done since he killed that dude on his birthday.

Much to the Demimondaines and Serriana's surprise, the young man had outlasted all of them. It was to the point where they were going to be late to the airport, so they put him out of the car.

Serriana thought about bringing Graham along so that she could kill him slowly, but admired his stamina and decided to toss him aside unharmed instead.

He stood on the curb and watched the limo pull out and head east on West 44th Street toward LaGuardia. "Left those bitches sore!" He bragged aloud, even though there was no one around to hear. He was feeling a sudden burst of strength and confidence.

Sitting inside the now silent recording studio, inside the silent hallway, inside the silent case, the Axe began to form back into a solid. The new soul was already near.

While they were all swapping body fluids, Serriana shared that Blue Oyster Cult was going to load into The Record Plant and start recording that evening.

Graham would have liked to stick around to meet them, but he was tired. He also wanted to pick up a new copy of On Your Feet or on Your Knees, their recently released live album.

The album cover was an artistic delight, He loved the way the limo and house were curved in to fit under the ominous clouds. He would have them sign it right under the band's name, on the lighter part of the sky.

Tomorrow would have to do. Now, he needed sleep. And sleep he did, without dreams or interruption.

He had a quick breakfast and then went out to buy On Your Feet or on Your Knees. Graham wanted a pristine cover for the members of Blue Oyster Cult to sign.

If things worked right, he could make it to a record store that opened early, the one on West 53rd Street, then get to The Record Plant in time to catch the band coming out.

Things did work right. Graham was waiting by the door when three of the band members and their producer exited, all upbeat about the session.

"Did you hear Buck play that solo? That was one hot fucking solo!"

He slipped the plastic wrap off of the album and politely asked for their autographs.

The producer, David Lucas, snapped pictures of Allen Lanier and both of the Bouchards signing the way cool cover.

"Is there any way that I can get Buck Dharma and Eric Bloom's signatures too?" He asked the producer. "Sure." Lucas, feeling generous, told him "They're still inside listening to the stuff we recorded last night.

I'll take you up there."

"Thanks!"

Lucas walked into the control room leaving Graham standing beside a small hallway. His eyes were drawn to the Gibson case leaning against the wall.

It was muffled, but he could hear music being pumped through the main control room speakers.

...seasons don't fear the Reaper.

The music stopped.

The control room door opened and the producer motioned Graham in.

"Hey Eric, go me a favor would you and sign my new friend's album?"

"Sure David, give it here." With a flourish he placed his name underneath the rest."

"Where's Buck?"

The singer replied. "He just stepped out, I think he's in the hall by the equipment now." Lucas waved Graham back through the door and into the hallway.

As Dharma was adding his signature, Shelly stepped in and bluntly announced, "Serriana's plane went down last night in east Texas! I just heard it on the news!" The engineer was drawn with despair. Then, a sudden look of relief ran across his face. "Buck." He offered quietly. "I shouldn't be saying this man, but you know that we really dodged a hard bullet here."

"Yea, Shelly, you are right as Hell about that!"

Graham Graves and Buck Dharma both heard the riff and looked toward the ES-335's case at the exact same time. The riff from last night started to pulse from it. Shelly, lost in his shock, did not hear the music at all. Buck picked up the case and handed it to Graham. "I think Serriana would want you to have this," he told the boy.

"Yes. She would." Graham opened the case and caressed the Axe. It was his now!

The engineer started to object, saying that the Axe was not Buck's property to give away. The look that Graham gave Shelly changed his mind. He stepped out of the way and allowed the boy to leave, taking the evil thing with him.

He played small private concerts with only one or two people attending. Graham always kept his audience screaming, but never for more.

Because there were no world tours, no stadium sized crowds, or no-hit records, Graham Grave's path of destruction went unnoticed by all authorities except God and Satan.

God started paying closer attention when He realized that He was beginning to lose some serious ground. He had created a lot of creatures, but His masterpiece, Mankind, was the only one that ever vexed Him.

From 1975 until 1984 the boy from Hell's Kitchen was always near the top of God's problem list. There were things

69

like galaxies colliding, black holes collapsing, and wars and famines to deal with. Then there was Graham Graves.

As soon as he first touched the dead black guitar case, Graham felt an amazing change come over him. The amount of hate and cruelty that he already carried inside increased one-hundred-fold.

He had never played any instrument before, but he knew that with this guitar it would make no difference. At midnight he would be the best ever, a virtuoso. A master of up close and personal pain.

Graham used the guitar only one time a day, He would start playing at eleven-fifty and go till twelve-ten. The piece was always introduced as *Last Song*, but he never played the same thing twice.

He left New York by train that afternoon, got off in Ohio and began to walk and hitch rides around the country.

Since there was no one left alive to tell about it, Graham's contribution to music never made it into history or lore.

He adapted the Axe's ability to slow down internal frequencies, allowing him move around without many taking notice, except for the twenty minutes each day that he played *Last Song*, then they noticed!

At first he stuck around the Midwest, working the Tri-state area of Indiana, Kentucky, and Ohio. The river valley was filled with solitary places that he could use for his performances.

There were lots of isolated homes and trailers to find an audience in. And there were boats, lots and lots of boats.

Around ten each night Graham would turn up his internal frequencies. He was usually already where he wanted to be, having spent the day watching from his slowed state.

Occasionally one of the victims would sense that they were being observed. It was always an Empath. They alone could even begin to feel the depth of his hostility. He enjoyed their discomfort. Their extra sensitivity to the world around them gave him more pleasure than usual when he played *Last Song* for them.

It was a typical Midwest night for Graham, the high-speed boat races under the Ohio river bridge by Madison, Indiana were the biggest thing going that July day. Thousands of people gathered underneath the span to watch the highly colored, very loud, fiberglass boats kick huge plumes of water into the air. They traveled so fast that they disintegrated if they hit the smallest of objects. The river was netted upstream the day before to minimize debris in the water.

Hoist Up Two was tied outboard of three similar sized boats at a pier located downstream of the race site. She was a classic from 1968.

At thirty-one feet, the fiber hulled Chris Craft used two Corvette engines to push her across the water. Lorrie liked to sleep in the upper bunk on the starboard side of the main cabin. The screened windows let in a pleasant breeze that lulled her into a state of altered consciousness. The rest of the crew had already left for the races. They went early to find a good place for the fireworks after, and to watch the stunt pilot fly below the bridge. She chose to rest up and go later.

Lorrie never made it. She did, however, get to hear the best guitar playing ever.

Tony was a used car salesman in Madison. He took a potential buyer out for a test drive in a Corvette and never showed up again. It was the end of a normal work day when the dealership's best salesman decided to shoot for one more sale.

The races where in town and the Corvette was back on the lot, Tony had requested some vacation time, so nobody even missed him for a couple of weeks. Graham had a soft spot for used car salesman and lawyers, so he cut Tony some slack, but not much.

He played to a couple on the Kentucky side of the river the next night and then did a three-night stand in Ohio.

Feeling very satisfied, Graham stood by an entrance ramp to I-70 West, the Axe slung over his shoulder with his thumb out.

This went on for nine years. Eventually the time to pass the Axe along arrived. Graham was one of the few allowed to live after his possession of it. Satan needed him for one more task, so Mr. Graves was spared.

"I want five thousand, cash."

"It's not worth fifty."

"Five thousand, nothing less."

"It smells like dead fish."

"Five thousand, don't make me say it again."

"Five thousand, that's a lot of money. Do you have some identification?"

"No."

The pawn shop owner took a closer look at the man standing in front of him. He capitulated. "Okay."

Graham came back to the pawnshop the following Wednesday. He watched intently as a white van parked in a space in front.

The driver carried a guitar case in. He came out twenty minutes later with the same case, shaking his left hand.

It took him a few tries to unlock the van's door.

Graham waited a minute then walked over.

He motioned for the driver to roll the window down.

"Is your name Martin?" he asked.

XVII
Cathy and Martin

Cathy was in a great mood! Finding the exact right gift for her husband had been difficult, but she had finally located it in a pawn shop a few blocks from the jewelry store she worked at. It was the perfect present for Martin to celebrate their fifteenth anniversary. A guitar!

She spotted it hanging in the window on her way to lunch. Martin was a pretty good guitarist and Cathy knew he preferred a Gibson over any other brand. There were three of them sitting on stands in his practice room, but none of them were as beautiful as the red one radiating its presence at her through the big glass window.

For an extra hundred bucks the guy behind the counter agreed to have her and Martin's initials etched on the back of the headstock, along with the wedding and anniversary dates. Cathy could have it home before the big day. It was so exciting!

She loved Martin dearly and knew that he would be thrilled with the gift.

The pawn shop owner called her and said that the guitar was ready to pick up.

She rushed right over from work.

After showing her the engraving for approval, he carefully placed it into its case.

"Your husband is going to be very pleased," he said. "I know," she answered. "This is the absolute best present I have ever found for him."

The owner was relieved when Cathy finally carried the instrument out the door. He couldn't believe that he had unloaded that piece of shit guitar. The damn thing wouldn't tune up properly, and the inside of the ratty case smelled like a dead fish. The only reason he had taken it in the first place was that the man selling it had made him very uncomfortable. The guy, skinny and mean looking, was steadfast in his demand of five-thousand dollars.

He was disgusted with himself for paying so much for the damn thing. But he would have paid twice as much to get that man out of his store.

He bought it, then stashed in the back room. His full intention was to toss it into the dumpster outback. He would take the loss and forget about it. Toss and loss, it was funny how those words rhymed and emphasized each other.

That night he received a call from the security company informing him that a fire alarm had went off in his building. He rushed down to find a firetruck sitting out front. The fireman standing by the door told him that even though there was a lot of smoke, there was no other sign of a fire. They were looking around but had not yet found the source of the sulfur smelling vapor that filled the shop.

After the fire department packed up and departed, the owner went around to assess the damage. That is when he discovered the Axe hanging front and center in the display window. His instinct cautioned that it was best to leave it there.

Driving home with the guitar in the back seat, Cathy found herself singing *Sympathy for the Devil* under her breath.

Not the biggest fan of the Rolling Stones, she surprised herself for knowing all of the words. The immaculate case faded and almost completely disappeared into the plush black leather seat. She hid the Axe in a storage space under the basement stairs. The secret gift was safe there.

Martin had no reason to look into it, at least not before their upcoming anniversary.

Before stowing it away, she examined the guitar one last time. The engraver had done a real fine job with the inscription. Using a Comic Sans font, he had cut two rows, each three-eighths of an inch high. Printed lengthwise between the tuning pegs, it read **CBJ & MLJ Forever.** Placed right beneath was the couple's wedding and fifteenth anniversary dates: 03-26-1974 / 03-26-1989

The body vibrated slightly and flushed to a deeper angry red. Filled in with a crisp white enamel paint, the carved numbers and letters seemed to absorb all sound and light. Complete black and absolute silence momentarily filled the room.

A bright flash from the headstock then blasted out like a white-hot torch,

Startled, Cathy almost dropped the Axe! Not wanting to take a chance on damaging the instrument, she quickly placed it back into the case.

As she did so, she noticed that the numbers and letters no longer showed in white relief. They were now a crisp funeral black.

Martin had a gig with his quartet that Friday night. The band had become popular with the college crowd and played many of the larger campuses around the state. This show was taking place at a college about fifty miles to the north. They had managed to get two shows out of the deal, one Friday night for the students and one late Saturday afternoon at a professor's retirement party. On impulse, Cathy asked for Friday afternoon and Saturday morning off. She was a valued employee so the owner of the jewelry store agreed. "I'll ask my son to fill in, he won't mind."

As she left his office, she heard her boss call out.

"Don, could you come in here for a minute please?"

"Sure, Dad, let me finish with this customer." Don loved making the sale and his dad, in that order.

The Heartbeats had rehearsed at Martin's house once a week until the bass player moved to a larger place with a rec room. They could leave the equipment set up, so the weekly practice was shifted to his new digs. Having not heard them for a while, she looked forward to listening to the new songs Martin told her about. Cathy loved Madonna and was anticipating The Heartbeats' version of *Like a Prayer.*

As a bonus to her surprise visit, Cathy had also booked a motel room for Friday night.

She and Martin could start celebrating their anniversary early. That thought also made her very happy.

It was a beautiful day to be driving. Cathy took back roads that cut through the Horicon Marsh. Miles and miles of flat water alive with feeding ducks and geese. Through the big windshield, a large afternoon sun warmed both her body and her soul.

In no time she found herself arriving at the college campus nestled firmly into the city's center. Following the signs, she pulled into the parking lot. At the far end she saw the band's van sitting in a loading zone. It was close to the double doors used to accommodate moving equipment through to the backstage area.

Two people were walking toward it, one was her husband, Martin, the other a young woman she did not know. They were laughing! They were FUCKING HOLDING HANDS!

Stunned, Cathy stopped the car. Martin, his attention completely focused on the pretty girl beside him, did not see his enraged wife parked just a few rows away. The couple climbed into the van's back area and pulled the doors shut.

Clutching the steering wheel so tightly that it felt like it might snap off in her hands, burning hot tears began to spill down her cheeks. Her first thought was to confront her husband and smash his face, but Cathy was not the hysterical type, nor did she like to argue. As if trapped in a thick, sticky web, she could only sit there as hurt and confusion pummeled at her very being. In twenty minutes, they emerged from the van. The girl straightened her blouse, kissed the cheater on the cheek and headed back into the building. Martin, with a smug self-satisfied look on his face, pulled a guitar case and an amp out, then followed.

As soon as her husband was out of sight, Cathy left the car and went over to the van. The doors were unlocked, In the cargo area the pungent smells of pot and salty sex were mixed together, making her slightly nauseous and even more angry.

She pulled out the two remaining guitar cases and returned to the car. After she tossed them in the trunk, she got behind the wheel, started the car and sped out of the lot.

A few minutes later Martin discovered the two instruments were missing. He looked around but saw no one moving about. Thinking that one of the other guys may have carried them inside, he rushed back to the stage area.

Somewhere in the middle of the Horicon Marsh, Cathy stripped the symbol of their love off of her finger and tossed it out the car window into a reed filled ditch. As the ring sank, a large fish saw the diamond flash and hit on the it, taking it down with a single swallow.

Back on campus, Martin was freaking out. The guitars had clearly been stolen. One of them was his favorite, left to him by his older brother, Mark. Mark died in early 1975 trying to save some civilians being overrun by the Vietcong.

As much as he hated to do it, he had to report the theft, otherwise the insurance company would not cover the loss. To his relief, security did not need to see inside the van. The pot smell would have caused him more trouble.

The gig sucked. Martin couldn't keep his head in the game. What was worse was that The Heartbeats had to stay and play again the next afternoon. The young lady that had given him so much pleasure earlier was bummed at his bad mood and told him she wasn't going to spend the night with him.

He called Cathy several times, but the phone just kept ringing. He finally gave up.

Back at their home in the basement, Cathy found some tools and made a few modifications to Martin's guitars. First she clipped the strings off. Then, starting on the rare 1969 Super 400 CES, she ball-peened the highly polished blond finish, smashed the gold-plated pick-ups, and sawed several deep cuts across the neck. It had been given to Martin by his older brother before he went to Vietnam and was killed, so she knew the damage would cause the cheating little bastard a lot of emotional pain. Good! Payback was a stone-cold bitch. The hammer was a Stanley and left an 'S' imprinted in the center of each perfect little dent. Cathy noticed this she and smiled with satisfaction. From the storage space under the steps, she could hear Mick singing faintly.

Let me introduce myself,
I'm a man of wealth and taste...

Picking up a large heavy pipe wrench, she turned on the Les Paul and bashed it into pieces the size of toothpicks.

She returned the destroyed guitars to their proper cases and then carried them upstairs and out to the enclosed front porch. There she placed them on the large hanging swing-chair.

Don, the jewelry store owner's son, normally did not work on Saturdays. He liked to stay out late on Friday nights and chase women. Even though Saturdays were usually busy and provided a lot of commissions, Don preferred to sleep in. But his dad's request was really an order, so there he was, hungover and a little pissed that he had to leave a good-looking woman's bed earlier. At least they were only open until twelve, he could go home and crash for the afternoon.

When Cathy arrived at seven-forty-five, he was pleasantly surprised. "I thought you were traveling out of town to listen to Martin's band?"

Don had been hot for Cathy from the very beginning, so he was more than glad to see her show up for work. She seemed happily married though, and had never give him reason to think an advance would be accepted. This morning she was wearing a widow black sweater and skirt. The slightly tight sweater accented the fullness of her breasts, the short skirt showed off her long legs.

"It didn't work out the way I planned," she answered.

"Martin had some other things going on."

He could tell that she was distracted. Being in sales, he was fairly observant and noticed right away that Cathy was not wearing her wedding ring.

Don could not remember ever seeing her without it. Strangely, the pale circle of skin that normally shows when someone removes a ring that's been worn a long time was not present. Her ring finger was the same shade as the rest. Concerned, he asked, "Are you okay?"

"Yes, Don, I'm fine."

It was easy to tell she wasn't. Wouldn't it be wonderful, Don thought to himself, if she were having marital problems? That would mean that maybe, just maybe, he would have a shot at getting between those beautiful legs. At the thought of having sex with her, he could feel himself becoming excited. It was a good thing he was standing behind the counter so she couldn't see him shifting around.

"Well, Cathy," he told her, "if you need anything, you just let me know."

"I will, thanks. You are a good friend." Turning away, she went into the back room to inspect some of the new pieces designed and built by the in-house staff.

Don watched her walking down the short hallway and seriously considered leaving the closed sign up and following her back. The old man would be royally pissed if he did that, so reluctantly he flipped the sign over and unlocked the door to open for business. She could feel Don's eyes sizing her up, so she put a little extra sway in her hips just to tease him.

Cathy usually found his blatant fascination with her humorous and a little annoying. But, right now she thought, if he came back and put a move on her, she would not resist. To tell the truth, she was a little disappointed when she heard him unlock the front door. It wasn't that Cathy really wanted Don, it was that she felt that if she should die suddenly, she did not want that lying bastard husband of hers to be the last man she had sex with.

Sitting at her desk, she slipped on a jeweler's glass and began to look over the new jewelry. No custom piece was delivered until Cathy or the store owner gave approval on the quality and workmanship. Gold and diamonds where her area of expertise, and knowing what the customers liked made her a lot of money. She was looking at, but not seeing the work in front of her. Instead, the scene with Martin and the college chick getting into the band's van played again and again in her head.

People started arriving, she could hear the chime each time the door opened. Various voices floated back to her from the front, including Don's.

Taking a minute before she went out to help, Cathy placed a call. She told the guy that answered that her pocketbook had been stolen and that it contained her license and a spare house key.

Worried that someone might come to the house and rob it, she asked if he could send someone over around one o'clock to re-key the door locks. He quoted a price and agreed to meet her at one.

It was a very busy morning, keeping both of them on the floor working with customers. Don was feeling very good about his chances with Cathy. She smiled at him a few times and when he brushed her hand while pouring her a cup of coffee, she didn't pull away. His excitement grew!

By eleven-ten, Don realized that he was having a record-breaking day in sales. Everyone he dealt with bought something. Cathy was having the same experience.

At eleven-forty, Dog walked in. Don's dreams for a hook-up with his sexy co-worker were suddenly dashed.

XVIII
The Ring's Journey

Out in the marsh, a proud father watched as his son reeled in a lunker bass. When they slit the fish's belly to clean it, they found the wedding ring. It was obviously expensive, a large diamond surrounded by several smaller ones on a thick gold mounting. Two names, Cathy and Martin, and the date 3-26-74 were inscribed on the inner band.

But by the time he got home and showed his wife his find, the engraving had completely vanished. The area where it had been was shiny and smooth. Puzzled about the missing inscription, he told her she could keep it if she wanted.

"Get rid of it!" She told him. "Sell it or throw it away, I don't care which!" Her voice dropped in both pitch and volume. "That ring has nothing but sadness attached to it."

"How could you know that?' he asked.

"How could you not?" she quickly replied, then turned her back on him and the damned ring. She felt an intense pity for the unfortunate soul that had worn it. The husband shrugged and stuck it back into his pant's pocket.

He would get for it what he could at the pawn shop when he went down to the city on Wednesday.

XIX
Dog

Dog was a well-known local musician. He fronted a heavy metal band called Roadkillers, screaming lyrics into a Shure ball mic and fast slamming power chords on a black Gibson ES-335 guitar. He had accrued a large number of tattoos and always stripped off his shirt during a show to reveal them.

Two large hissing snakes faced each other across his chest. The left bicep had the likeness of a tan and black German Shepherd. It was his very first tattoo, in memory of Gandalph, a dog that once saved his life. On the right side was a drawing of his current canine, a Doberman named Sniper. They were the reason he was nicknamed Dog. Inked on his back was a picture of a Gibson J-200 and the Gibson ES-335 he played in Roadkillers.

His upper body was well sculpted, the result of intense daily work-outs. A few years back the band scored big with an album called *Psychotics on the Highway*. When asked during an interview how it felt to be on the way to the top of the metal heap, Dog told the journalist, "I consider the music that Roadkillers play as an extremely aggressive form of rock-and-roll. Still, it does feel pretty damned good,"

Women loved and lusted for Dog.

Cathy remembered Dog from before his metal days. Then he was Alex, with no multicolored ink pictures covering his back, biceps, and chest. She and Martin had hired his band to play their wedding reception. Even back then Alex was a hit with the ladies. The maid-of-honor, her best friend Cindy, and one of the other bridesmaids left with him at the end of the evening. When the two friends got together after her honeymoon to chat, Cindy made Cathy blush describing the threesome's sexual encounter.

"Well come on," Cathy said as she poured each of them a glass of wine, "Start at the beginning and don't leave out a single dirty detail."

A couple of years later Alex showed up at one of Martin's gigs. During the second set Martin invited him to sit in with The Heartbeats for a few songs. "I don't have an axe with me," Alex told Martin. "No problem, you can play the Super 400." Alex strummed a few chords to get a feel for the action. "This is one sweet guitar, Martin. What songs do you guys want to try?"

Out in the audience Cathy listened as Alex's playing transformed the band from really good to great. Seeing him again caused her to think of Cindy's naughty escapade. It made her more than a little horny. Martin got a wild ride later that night.

That was what seemed like forever ago. Cindy had married and moved on, and now Dog was standing there in front of her holding a watch. "Hey Cathy, long time no see. I didn't know you worked here."

Hello Alex, it's hard to believe, but I have been here for over nine years." She looked down at the timepiece. "That's a beautiful watch, what do you want done with it?"

86

"I need to get it repaired and cleaned. I was jumping around on stage and cracked the face against a mic stand. It's probably full of crud too because I sweat a lot."

"We can replace the broken crystal and clean it, but not today. We close at noon. How about Tuesday?"

"No problem, the band is taking a few weeks off before we start recording again so I'm in town for a while."

Cathy took the watch to the back and wrote up a work order. As she was tearing off the perforated claim check a thought crossed her mind.

"Your watch will be ready after one o'clock on Tuesday. You will need this to pick it up." She handed him the small numbered slip.

"Thanks." Dog took the slip and tucked it into his shirt pocket. "It's been lucky for me, I'll see you Tuesday."

You don't know how lucky, she thought. She spoke quickly before he had a chance to leave. "Say Alex, you wouldn't be in the market for a guitar, would you?"

"I'm always looking for a good guitar, what have you got?"

"It's an older Gibson that Martin wants to get rid of. It's very pretty and I know that he is willing to deal on it."

"It's good to see you two still together, how long has it been?"

"Fifteen years tomorrow."

"Is he still playing with The Heartbeats?"

"Oh yes, his band is doing very well on the college circuit. He has three other guitars and doesn't need this one." She thought about the two smashed Gibsons sitting on the porch swing and almost laughed. "So, are you interested?"

87

"Sure, when can I take a look?"

"You know, today would be good, maybe around three."

"Okay, where is it?"

"It's at our house, I'll give you the address." She jotted the street and number down on a post-it note.

"Here."

Don watched Cathy write down and hand Dog her address, his heart sank.

Out in the parking lot, Dog glanced at the post-it, the address was not far, maybe ten minutes away.

There was plenty of time for a work out and a shower before three.

Remembering Cathy and Martin's wedding brought back the night of sweaty bliss with the two ladies that he had taken back to his room after the gig. What were their names? Twila for sure and maybe Cindy?

Of course he had noticed that Cathy was looking fine and that she was not wearing her wedding ring. There were many reasons that would explain why she did not have it on, and the conversation led him to believe the couple was still together. He was looking forward to seeing how Martin was holding up after all these years. He was also hoping the guitar for sale was going to be something special, maybe that 400 CES Martin had let him play once.

In the car he plotted a route to the gym that would take him by a bank, he wanted some cash just in case he decided to buy the guitar.

The locksmith arrived at one as promised. It didn't take him long to re-key the house and garage door locks, setting them up so that a single key worked on all three. Cathy made another appointment for later in the week to install an electronic security and alarm system.

She thanked him and gave him a nice tip for his efforts.

After the locksmith's vehicle backed out of the driveway, Cathy went to the basement and tripped the breaker that supplied power to the garage. She then went upstairs and drew a bath, letting the hot water soak away the built-up stress. Instead of being upset with Martin for being unfaithful, she found herself anticipating Dog's visit.

That brought the guitar she wanted to get rid of back to mind. She wondered of the engraving on the headstock would bother Dog. She was sure it could be easily removed. Climbing out of the tub, she dried and dressed in an oversized t-shirt and tight jeans. When she opened the door to the storage closet, she did not see the Gibson guitar case. Her first thought was, where did it go? As she stood there it began to take its dark shape, quickly becoming solid again. No longer surprised by the weirdness that surrounded the instrument, she pulled the case off of the shelf and took it up to the living room.

A little after three, the doorbell chimed; Cathy's heart started to beat faster.

Dog stood on the enclosed porch and pushed the button for the doorbell. He could sense movement inside the house.

As he glanced around, he noticed the two guitar cases on the swing. Martin must have set them out to load up for a gig. He wondered what they were and would have opened the cases to see had not Cathy just then answered the door. Damn she looked good! That Martin was one lucky bastard.

"Hey Alex, come on it."

"Hello, Cathy. You know I haven't been called Alex for years now." He stepped through the door as he spoke. "Well, except for Mom."

"Sorry, the last time I saw you, you were Alex. Do you want me to call you Dog?"

He took a long look at the beautiful woman standing in front of him. "Stick with Alex if you like, I don't mind. So, where is this guitar that you have for sale?" Cathy led him into the front room. "It's in here." In another room a phone was ringing but Cathy ignored it. "Go ahead and get that," he told her. "That's alright, I know who it is and they'll call back later." She pointed to the extremely black case sitting on the coffee table. "This is it."

Before Dog even touched it, he felt its dark power starting to suck him in.

It was the reddest red he had ever seen and in mint condition. He examined the body, looked down the neck and checked the serial number on the headstock. From that he was able to figure out the year it was built.

"1963, that's really sweet." he said aloud. There wasn't a single scratch, mark, or even a fingerprint on it anywhere. The neck was perfect, the action explosive, the tone commanding. He was completely hooked after just a few chord strums. Cathy moved to his side as he inspected the set-up. When Dog commented on the serial number, she was relieved to see the engraving no longer existed on the headstock.

"How much?" he demanded, ready to pay whatever was asked.

"You can't buy this guitar," she told him. "You have to earn it."

Dog put down the Axe and wrapped his arms around her. Their first kiss was as close to Heaven as Hell would allow it to be.

The phone began to ring again. Fifty-some miles away on the other end of the line, Martin stood holding a phone receiver wondering why Cathy wasn't answering his calls.

The drummer poked his head through the motel room's door. "Come on Martin, we've got to go set up, we start at five you know.

At eight o'clock with the miserable gig now behind them, the band tore down and packed the equipment into the van. Martin was eager to leave and could barely contain himself while they gassed up for the return trip. A car pulled up to the pump beside them, the pretty co-ed from yesterday was driving. The bass player went over and spoke with her then came back to the van. "Hey guys, I'm staying here tonight, she'll take me home tomorrow." He jabbed Martin in the arm. "See you later, buddy."

As the car rolled away with the bass player in the passenger seat, the girl gave Martin a little smile and a middle finger wave good-bye. Rain began to fall.

It was well after eleven and storming hard when Martin finally pulled the van into his driveway. Exhausted from the gigs, the difficult drive back, and the loss of his guitars, he wanted a hot shower and rest.

Most of all he needed his wife to hold and comfort him.

The house was dark, Cathy was probably already asleep. He punched the remote for the garage door but it did not open. Damn it!

What else could go wrong? Running from the driveway to the covered porch, he got soaked by the cold deluge. He found out what else could go wrong when he tried the front door key.

Flipping an outside switch to turn the porch light on, he checked to make sure he was using the right key. He was. Martin could hear the bell sounding as he pushed and re-pushed the button, becoming almost frantic when Cathy did not let him in.

Then he saw the two guitar cases sitting on the swing. Shock was already starting to set in as he opened the one for the CES.

In the bedroom the lovers slipped apart when the doorbell started ringing. "Sounds like Martin is home," Alex whispered to Cathy. "Are you going to answer?"

"Hell no!" She pulled him on top and guided him back inside. The bell stopped. A few moments later they heard her husband's primal scream. It filled Cathy with great joy to hear it. She started thrusting herself harder against Dog.

Right before mid-night, Dog left Cathy's bed to go play the Axe. As he walked out of the bedroom, she saw that the ES-335 tattoo on his back had turned from coal-black to blood-red.

Sunday morning was clear and cold. Thin sunshine filled the kitchen with light. Martin, the guitar cases, and the van were gone. Cathy was humming as she made breakfast for the two of them.

"Did I earn the guitar last night?"

"It was a great down payment, honey, but you have to do one more thing for me."

"Name it."

She nibbled on his ear, then told him what else she wanted.

"No problem, I know a guy that can help. I'll make the call right now." Dog picked up the extension phone and dialed seven digits. "Hello, hey man, this is Dog."

He listened for a moment, then spoke, "I'm doing great, you know lots of pussy and lots of guitars. Listen, Graham, I need a small favor, and you are just the man to do it."

Dog listened again, then spelled out his request. He hung up, looked a Cathy and smiled. "It's set up baby." Cathy smiled back. "After it's done the guitar is all yours."

"He said two or three days, Graham is a very reliable guy. Now, I know that I have to wait to own the guitar, but do I have to wait on the pussy too?"

"No, let's go back upstairs, or right here if you feel like it."

Dazed and confused, Martin took the cases and left. Luckily, he had some dry clothes in the van to change into.

Drinking coffee alone at a twenty-four-hour café, he started to piece things together. The only way Cathy could have had possession of the guitars was if she had been on the college campus. That meant she had seen had seen him with the girl!

Today was their fifteenth anniversary and here he was on the total outs, his perfect life ruined by a meaningless fuck.

He was starting to get pissed about the massive damage to the guitar his older brother had left him. It was downright cruel of her to ruin his most cherished possession. Growing anger caused him to ball up his fists, that bitch was going to pay dearly!

First he needed a place to stay. Figuring the bass player would be back home by late morning, he decided he would drive over there. He parked on the street in front of the house to wait. Chilled to the bone from the soaking, he let the van run with the heater going full blast. The exhaustion caught up with him and he soon fell into a troubled and uncomfortable sleep. The bass player showed up around noon. He set Martin up in a spare bedroom and spent the afternoon bragging about the great sex he and the girl had the night before.

It only served to make Martin feel even more miserable.

XX
The Ring Returns

The pawnbroker looked the ring over one more time. He thought that he had recently seen this piece but he could not place it. Excusing himself to the gentleman that brought it in, he went into the backroom to check the hot sheet. If a ring this beautiful and expensive was a stolen item, it would surely be listed. It was not. The story the guy was feeding him about finding it when he gutted a fish did not seem plausible. To be fair though, the pawn shop owner had heard stranger things. He decided to buy it, if he could get it for anything less than three grand.

"I can offer you fifteen hundred for it."

"Come on man, you can do better than that," countered the fisherman. "Another five hundred and it's yours."

The pawnbroker hesitated a bit, like he really had to consider the deal. "You'll have to let me make a copy of your ID just in case."

"Not a problem, I know it's not stolen."

A short while later the thrilled fisherman left the pawnshop with a couple of thousand dollars in his pocket.

The ring was put on immediate display. It was a bargain at seventy-five hundred.

Twenty minutes after the fisherman vacated it, a white van pulled into the parking spot in front of the pawn shop. Martin had no choice but to sell his last guitar. He was short on cash and needed a few bucks to get by. During the previous two days, Cathy had frozen the checking and savings accounts, leaving him no access and dead broke. He cursed himself for letting her control their finances. She was putting his nuts in a vice, making his life a total Hell. All over a little strange. To tell the truth, he had starting cheating on her a few years into the marriage. He never worried about what would happen if he got caught because he never thought he would get caught.

Now he was reduced to selling his last guitar. It was the least expensive one, but he should still be able to get a thousand bucks, or maybe a little more for it. Martin had been in the shop one time before. Last year when the bass player was looking for different guitar, they had found one there for a decent price.

Getting out of the van he did a look around. Maybe he was being just a little paranoid, but he had a strong feeling that someone was watching him. No one appeared to be paying any particular attention though, so he shrugged it off and went inside.

The shop owner, busy placing something in the main display case looked up and asked, "How may I help you?"

There right in front of him, perched on a red satin cloth, sat Cathy's wedding ring. She had spent weeks designing it. The diamond's sparkle taunted him. On his left hand, the thick tri-gold band he wore matched it perfectly. "Let me see that ring!" he insisted.

"I see you have an eye for quality," The pawnbroker ventured as he handed the ring to Martin.

His hand shook as he looked it over. He saw right away that the inscription was gone. The inner band was as smooth as if it had never been cut into. He passed it back to the owner, his heart shattering into thousands of tiny pieces.

The tri-gold band on Martin's finger began to heat up, searing into his finger and causing him to quickly yank it off and drop it. He could not believe what he was seeing, the ring glowed red hot. When it cooled, Martin picked it back up. The inside engraving was now gone. It was as if it were never there. Knowing that his life was now completely ruined, he offered the wedding band to the pawnbroker. "What can you give me for this?"

He was still shaking when he got back to the van.

His ring finger was blistered and hurt like a bitch. It took three times to shove the key into door lock. At least, he reasoned, he now had some cash and was able to hang onto the guitar. That meant he could make some money down the road with The Heartbeats, after his burnt finger healed. He inserted the key into the ignition and started the engine.

Before he could place the vehicle in gear he was startled by a tapping on the window. A skinny, mean looking man was staring in. He motioned for Martin to roll down the window. "Is your name Martin?"

"Yes, it is, why?"

"I have something from Cathy for you."

"What's that?"

"This." The skinny man pulled open the door and violently jerked him out. He twisted Martin around, took the guitar player's blistered left hand and placed it palm down against the jamb. Then, he slowly pushed the van door shut until it latched.

Graham Graves left Martin hanging in the closed door. He turned around and walked away from the now totally fucked musician without looking back. When the screams reached full volume, he began to laugh. He had to admit, it was a pretty good way to end his career of evil service.

A couple of blocks down he turned into a blind alley behind a music store.

He knocked on the door. It opened. A soft and smeared crimson light silhouetted the large figure that answered.

Graham spoke. "I've done everything that you have asked. May I come in now?"

The large figure stepped aside and Graham entered into the soft and smeared crimson light.

XXI
Cathy and Dog

Roadkillers' next big hit, *Most Wicked Bitch,* launched them into metal super-stardom. The huge crowds went insane at the opening riff and started singing loudly along with the first line, "You're petty and you're cruel and that's why I like you."

Cathy, always backstage during the shows, knew that Dog wrote it as a love song especially for her. It was her total favorite.

Once every performance she joined the band on stage and sang *Sympathy for the Devil.* The Rolling Stones loved Roadkillers' version and gave them full permission to use it on their new project. Both Keith and Mick showed up at the recording session to sing back-up vocals.

Dog was at home on the road, so was Cathy. After living her life in one city and holding the same job for many years, she enjoyed the constant travel and new places.

Although not the band's manager, she served as the de facto public relations person. Cathy had been top in sales at her old job, and knew how to get people to say yes.

Hotel personnel, limo drivers, venue managers, and roadies alike were happy to deal with the beautiful and charming woman. Almost all of them, male or female, wanted to have sex with her. None of them ever did, but just the feeling of the possibility was addicting. She worked hard to ensure everything was always in place for a successful show.

She also knew lots of dealers, pimps and other nefarious people. The band and their guests were always well supplied with the drugs and hookers they used to relax after an intense gig.

Cathy did not indulge in the drugs or debauchery, she was more than satisfied with Dog. Physically he gave her everything that she needed. Mentally she was a self-sufficient island, completely secure within herself. Dog often did participate in the after-show parties, but Cathy did not care.

Her heart had been hardened against love, or anything even close to it.

The girl that at one time would have never hurt even a fly was now completely cruel and callous.

XXII
The Axe

The only thing Dog cared about more than Cathy was the Axe. He needed Cathy, but he NEEDED the Axe. It was the very center of his existence.

With it he led the band across eleven years of major popularity. Their albums went gold and then platinum, all of the shows sold out. The merchandise income alone made them very rich.

Guitar buffs quickly noticed that Dog was wielding the same ES-335 that carried rock star Rusty Collins and then later, country queen Serriana, to world-wide prominence.

Like a real star is sustained by its own gravity, the evil and bad intent within the Axe's orbit kept it fueled.

Many an article in magazines like Guitar World and Guitar Player was written speculating on the instrument's history.

The serial number was known, so they all were able to determine the date of manufacture, but not a single author could actually track how the guitar had traveled from star to star, or account for its long absences from the public scene. When asked how he ended up with it, Dog would only state that he earned it by doing a favor.

The mystery continued.

The attempts to steal it were continuous. Private collectors all over the world coveted the guitar and offered huge amounts of money to anyone that could procure it, legally or otherwise.

A few came close. The law never heard about those attempts, so they were never charged with anything.

They simply disappeared.

The guitar would let the would-be thief open the case and get a good look that usually included verifying the serial number. They were always disappointed in how bland it appeared up close.

Then Dog would make his presence known.

For Cathy, punishing them was always a high-point in her day. The word 'mercy' was missing from her dictionary. While the rest of the band was getting high and screwing, she was busy making the thieves very sorry that they ever tried to steal the Axe.

Roadkillers were doing a major show in Indianapolis, Indiana. It was the kick-off for the year 2000 tour. Their new album, *Turn Up the Malice*, was ready for release. The band played the entire thing live, note for note.

> *I like to watch the flowers die,*
> *Watch them wilt and turn brown.*
> *I like to watch the flowers die,*
> *They never make a sound.*
> *The sun is shining down,*
> *Oh Lord, the rain is pouring down.*

As the last lyric from the song reverberated away, Dog exited the stage. Holding the Axe up high using his left hand, he waved at the fans with his right. The star hit a hidden opening in the jet-black stage curtains and vanished from the crowd's sight.

He stood back stage, gulping down water to hydrate, waiting a few minutes before going back out to play the encore song, *Most Wicked Bitch*.

Dog didn't make the encore. A major vessel in his head burst and flooded his brain with blood. Later, one of his doctors equated it with a fire hose filling a five-gallon bucket.

Cathy took charge just as soon as she saw her lover fall.

Within ten minutes, Dog was in an ambulance being transported to the nearest hospital. She was riding in the back with him. The Axe sat on the floor toward the rear. The EMTs had at first objected to Cathy bringing the filthy guitar case along. But, after she spoke to them quietly for a moment, they gave in.

"You can't bring that ma'am, its dirty and may cause the patient to get an infection."

Cathy chose honey to get her way. "Do this for me guys, I will make it worth your while later, I promise you."

When Dog went down, the Axe dropped out of his hand and landed on the floor a few feet from him. As Cathy issued orders to get help, she scooped it up and returned it to the case. She saw right away that the color had faded and that three of the corroded strings were broken. There where scratches and cracks all over. The pick-ups had become loose and rattled.

For no reason, she turned it over and looked at the back of the headstock. Engraved there in hard white relief and Comic Sans font was her long ago dedication to Martin. It looked brand new.

She understood.

Thirteen hours after Dog dropped to the back stage floor, his shallow and irregular breathing stopped. Because he died in a state that he did not reside in, an autopsy was required by law. The cause of Dog's death was attributed to a cerebellum vascular accident. After the cause of death was determined, his body was taken to the Flanner and Buchanan funeral home for cremation.

There would be no memorial service.

When they heard of Dog's death, a couple of fans realized that this tragedy could present the perfect opportunity to grab the extremely valuable Axe. They stood outside of the hospital with hundreds of other Roadkillers fans and then followed Dog's hearse to the funeral home on South Market Street. They watched Cathy leave her limo and carry the case with her into the building. The amount of money that that guitar was worth made all options available to retrieve it viable.

Cathy was waiting in a small hallway when she heard the two men enter the facility through a side door. She stood quietly and listened to their conversation. It did not take her long to realize they were there to steal the Axe. They would, she could tell, use violence if necessary to get it.

The few moments it took them to get their bearings and check their weapons allowed her time to slip into the working area of the funeral home. She made her way to the dock. A beautiful walnut casket sat there with shipping instructions taped to it. She did not know where Osgood, Indiana was, nor did she care. She just wanted to hide the Axe. She opened the casket and managed to fit the case underneath a young man's embalmed body. The Axe's frequencies immediately slowed and once again it became invisible to human beings.

She closed the heavy lid, then proceeded to one of the grief rooms. That is where they found her, alone. The two men made the big mistake of thinking that they had the advantage.

Cathy let one of them slap her a couple of times and make her lip bleed. It hurt a little more than she expected, but the pain was delicious. When the other guy flashed a knife, she pretended to be frightened and gave in.

"It's in the embalming room, please don't hurt me!" The stainless-steel room gave her every weapon she could want to deal with them. It took about thirty minutes to make them pay. She would have liked to have had more time, but she did have a cremation to arrange.

Meanwhile, the walnut casket was loaded into a hearse to be delivered to Neal's Funeral Home in a small town seventy some miles southeast of Indianapolis. Cathy completed the financial transaction and received heartfelt sympathies from the mortician's staff.

She then returned to the dock, but the casket was gone.

Strangely, she felt no need to pursue and retrieve it.

She shrugged and went to look for the two EMTs. Cathy was horny and wanted to keep the promise that she had made to them when they let her bring the Axe along to the hospital.

Three days later the mortician needed to use one of the refrigerated drawers. He was shocked to find two naked men stacked inside of it. Their blood had been drained out through the hundreds of deep little cuts sliced into each body. The shocked looks on their faces showed that they had suffered a great deal of pain.

As Neal's funeral director checked that Mr. Foamer was indeed inside the walnut casket, the hearse driver stood close by and peered intently over his shoulder. Everything looked fine, although the body was shifted around, probably from the drive. The director put it into the proper hands across the chest repose and closed the lid.

"You must have had to really hit the brakes on the way down here," the director commented.

The driver looked confused. "What makes you say that?"

"The way the body was shifted."

"That couldn't have caused it, I didn't make any hard stops at all. Let me tell you though, that is one heavy fucking casket."

"Well, it is made of walnut."

"It's heavy even for walnut. It was hard to push the gurney it was on and when we placed it in the back the hearse's tires all flattened a little. It looks normal, so I thought there must be a really fat person or something else inside of it."

"We just checked, I didn't see anything. Did you?" the funeral director asked.

"Nope," the driver answered, "and Mr. Foamer sure as the Hell ain't fat."

XXIII
Marshall Gets the Call

Marshall King was loath to leave the Seattle area, he loved being there and it was the only place in the world that he felt entirely comfortable and safe.

The feeling that his happy way of life was coming to an end had been building for months. Now the time had arrived for Marshall to abandon his adopted home and go do battle with the Devil. The bass player knew his chances of returning were damn near non-existent. The Creator needed His lead soldier to destroy the object that was bringing so much darkness and pain into the world.

After completing the last recording project under contract, Marshall sold the studio and cutting-edge gear. His house, sitting on the opposite side of the five-acre property, was sold as well. All of the furniture and cars went out the door during a complete estate sale. Two big collectors, Steven Stills and Rick Nielsen, bought all of his guitars. Neil Young ended up with most of the amplifiers, including the JMT45 signed by Who bassist John Entwistle. Memorabilia from the years of working with rock and roll stars got auctioned off for top dollar.

When Marshall departed Whidbey Island for the last time, the only things he took onto the ferry with him were the Fender Jazz Master bass and a small suitcase. The twenty-four hundred or so mile journey to the battlefield would take him several days.

The bass and suitcase were stored in the outside lower luggage compartment of the bus Marshall was rolling steadily eastward on. It was making continuous progress along State Road 30 in Iowa. The fields shimmered from an early fall heat wave that was scorching the Midwest.

It had been a very long time since Marshall rode on a Greyhound. The last time one picked him up at a dirt crossroads in Montana and carried him all the way to Seattle. As soon as the City of Flowers appeared through the bus's window, Marshall knew that it was where he truly belonged.

This trip Marshall sat all alone in the back. Sensing his inner turmoil, the other passengers gave him a wide berth. A drunk stumbled on board during the stopover in Le Grand and sat down beside the bass player. He was in a complete alcoholic fog. Still, it only took a few seconds for him to move away and find a different seat. Using a Triple A map to check the route, Marshall figured that with the remaining stops and transfers he would reach his destination in about twelve hours, early on the morning of the eleventh. It would be best to eat at the upcoming station and then get some sleep on the next leg of the trip.

He would need the strength.

XXIV
Preparation

The cemetery sat alongside a seldom traveled county road southwest of Osgood, Indiana. It contained the remains of many small-town citizens and farming community members that had once lived in the area. Covering about nine acres, it was hilly and rocky with the poor and the prominent buried randomly alongside each other. Death, if nothing else, is the great equalizer. The stones rose above the uncut grass at all angles, shifted by the earth's constant upheavals from the annual freezing and thawing. They were as different from each other as the people beneath them, some exquisite, some shoddy and broken.

It was a mid-September day and one of the underground occupants, Dan Gilland, was receiving special attention from the Almighty Powers; Above and Below.

While on earth, Dan had been a Baptist preacher. One hot July Sunday in 1934, young Jake Foamer acted up during the evening service. The preacher, never tolerant of an interruption, slapped the nine-year-old boy sharply upside of the head with a copy of the Good Book. A short while later Jake began to complain of a headache.

He then began to cry and say that he was seeing bright lights. He started to throw up, lapsed into unconsciousness and died. Young Jake's last breath was taken in a back pew in a House of God. His mother was weeping as she held him tightly in her arms.

The minister was forgiven by the Foamer family, but not by the law. Convicted of manslaughter, Dan Gilland went to prison for just over six and a half years. During his incarceration he was credited for bringing many souls to Jesus.

His body now lay only two rows away from the forever nine-year-old Jake.

God and the Devil agreed that Dan was an acceptable referee for the event.

It was not a *The Devil Went Down to Georgia* playoff with screeching violins, it was an all-out battle with a lot of innocent casualties.

The Axe was tucked into the coffin that held the body of little Jake's brother's great grandson, John. It was now buried in the Foamer family plot. The ground over John's grave remained bare. Interred into an extra deep grave in the late spring of 2000, the vault was still settling. The mowing crew continued to layer fresh dirt on the top. Even though it was over-seeded each time it was leveled out, the grass refused to grow.

John Foamer, in his mid-twenties when he passed, did not go to heaven. The gravedigger felt compelled to take extra steps to protect this particular plot. He used a John Deere 40 with the backhoe attachment to dig the hole an extra three feet deep. The idea came from a book he once read. It suggested that bank robber John H. Dillinger's grave was nine feet deep and partially filled with debris to make it difficult to dig up.

Someone at one time had very skillfully altered the famous logo on the green and yellow wheeled tractor. Whoever did it perfectly matched the size, font and color using the words Gravedigger 40 to cover the single word Deere. The motto now read: Nothing Runs Like a Gravedigger 40. On the bright yellow deer logo, an X was drawn where the eye would be to indicate that the animal was dead.

Before he refilled the deep hole, the gravedigger made a quick trip to the junk yard. There he picked up a truck's bed full of broken glass, rusty wire, and nasty bits of sharp metal. Upon returning to the grave site, he shoveled half of it directly on top of the cement vault. The rest of the dangerous mix was added to the fill at random.

XXV
Buddy Rich

Satan reached out to Buddy Rich. "Hey, I'm putting together a concert and I want you to play. We rehearse on the ninth and tenth, then open on the eleventh. You'll dig all the players."

Buddy replied, "Thanks for thinking of me, but do we really have to practice for two days?"

Satan explained to the drummer. "We're gonna have five different lead guitar players." He then listed their names. "You see the trouble is, Buddy, there is only one Axe for them to play, so we have to work with them individually."

Buddy thought it over. "Okay, I'll do it, but you know how I feel about fucking practice. By the way are you going to play or just listen?"

"I'm jumping in on the harmonica!"

"What the fuck, Satan? You can't play the harmonica worth a damn."

"Buddy, you are very lucky that I love you."

XXVI
The Rehearsal

Deep in the ground of central Indiana, the Axe started powering up as Marshall King approached from the west. Even Buddy was impressed with the line-up. The band would be fronted one player at a time by a different disciple of Satan's Guitar.

Rusty Collins kicked the rehearsal off, then Spike got his chance to shine. Third in line, Serriana, took the stage in full glory with her accessories, the Demimondaines.

Graham Graves played solo, he neither wanted or needed accompaniment. He was able to deliver the pain directly and personally. His set only lasted twenty minutes, but that's all Graham ever needed.

Dog took it home with a highly aggressive rock-and-roll set.

They were ready for the showdown.

XXVII
Cathy and Martin
The End of Love

Cathy was called up to sing only one song, *Sympathy for the Devil*. She was fairly new to Hell, having died on September 11th of 2000, exactly one year to the day. Returning to her home town after Dog's death in Indianapolis, she moved into a condo on the harbor. One Saturday morning she decided to visit her old place of employment.

Dog's lucky watch crystal had been re-broken when the vascular accident put him down hard on the floor. She decided to have it cleaned and repaired. The son was now in charge. His dad, Cathy's former boss, had retired and moved south for the warmer climate and tax advantages.

Don was thrilled to see her walk in that morning. As she leaned in close to explain what she needed done to the watch, Don felt himself getting hard. She noticed and smiled.

Five minutes later the entrance bell chimed. Don and Cathy looked toward the door. A familiar person stood there, he was obviously destitute and his left hand was drawn into a claw.

"Why hello, Martin." She looked him over, her eyes sparkled at his derelict appearance. "I hear you had to leave The Heartbeats. I'm so sorry." The sarcasm oozed from her voice."

"Hello, Cathy." He gave the son a small head nod.

"Don." He stepped toward the pair.

"What a surprise to see you! What brings you here?"

"Well, I have something for you." He proceeded to pull a switchblade knife and savagely attack Cathy and Don.

Martin sat on the floor in pools of their blood and calmly waited for the police to arrive. Because they were still alive, Cathy was surprised that Keith and Mick were at Roadkillers' rehearsal. Both of them were on everybody's dead pool list. No one figured that either one of them would have ever make it to fifty-eight. There was talk of one last Rolling Stones tour, surely the boys were getting too old to rock-and-roll.

Backstage after the rehearsal, Cathy complimented Satan on his harmonica playing.

"Kissing ass are we, Cathy?" Buddy wanted to know. "I only heard two or three good notes the whole time, and I'm sure that they were by accident."

"Shut up, Buddy. Can't you see that I've make a good impression on this lady here? I'm feeling lucky."

"You're going to need a lot more than luck to handle this lady. Are you sure you're up to it?"

"Buddy! Shut! Up!"

XXVIII
The Pawns Are in Place

Marshall arrived in Osgood at four-fifty-two in the AM. The bus dropped him off just south of the railroad tracks, near the center of town on State Road 421. He retrieved his possessions, stretched and looked around. The driver clicked the left blinker on and smoothly pulled the thirty-eight-thousand-pound vehicle back onto the southbound highway. Next stop, Versailles. Marshall looked across the street and saw a bread shop named The Damm Bakery. Looking back over his shoulder he realized that he was standing on the sidewalk right in front of The Damm Theater. Could his life get any stranger?

Sugar and caffeine seemed like a good idea. He went over to the shop and entered. Painted on the door glass in sharp colored green and white slanted text was the come on: *'Best Damm Donuts In Town!'*

How could he refuse that?

Marshall consumed a half-dozen assorted and drank several cups of coffee.

One more sugary bite and one more scalding sip and then he needed to be on the move. The sun would rise at six-twenty-two; it was important to be close to the cemetery then. The empty cup got tossed in the trash and the crumbs sticking to his four-day-old beard got brushed off with the back of his sleeve. It was time. Suitcase and guitar in hand, Marshall walked off to his fate. He wondered, should I stop and pray?

God had spelled everything out very clearly during the cross-country bus ride. Marshall was told that he was going to see the demise of thousands of people. He would be required to stand there and witness each and every one of them die, without resistance or complaint.

For God to win this confrontation Marshall could not flinch or move. He could not protest. He could not ask for it to be stopped.

He was allowed only silent tears.

There seemed to be no need to go over it again.

Anyway, God was busy enough this morning. He followed Railroad Avenue to the southwest and out of town. Each step toward the cemetery became increasingly difficult. Gravity was getting stronger as Marshall moved toward the Axe. It was tough going, but he was on the cemetery boundary at sunrise.

XXIX
The Referee

From among the tombstones the sounds of a band tuning up floated toward Marshall. A man wearing a prison uniform and holding an oversized Bible was blowing on a pitch pipe. The strings and horns slewed around as they sought to match the 440-cycle tone, Reverend Dan Gilland had three responsibilities as referee, He was to ensure the band stayed in tune. If they slipped out, God gained points. He was also to determine when it was time to change the musicians and lead player.

His biggest responsibility was to keep an eye on Marshall and drop the red flag attached to his belt should the bass player show the smallest sign of giving up.

Another typical day in America. The fall weather was good, people all across the land were flying in airplanes. They were going to work in tall buildings.

XXX
First Up, Rusty Collins

Marshall recognized Rusty's chops. He stepped onto the sacred ground and saw that Collins and the band were set up in-between the gravestones. There was no stage.

Buddy Rich's drums sat on a short riser supported by the poured cement covers for burial vaults. He was clearly having a good time.

Rusty Collins stared directly at Marshall King and demanded. "You owe me fifteen-hundred dollars! Clam, clam, clam motherfucker. That's fifteen-hundred bucks." The ES-335 was just as shabby and out of tune as Marshall remembered it to be. Rusty was playing it with only four grungy strings intact. The first E and G were broken.

"Your harmonica player sucks, Collins. I thought you only let professionals in your band."

Buddy Rich spoke up, "I'm with you on that one."

"Thanks, Buddy. You were excellent in spite of the bad harp playing."

"You know Marshall, I've been covering for fuck-ups like Him my whole career."

Satan got very pissed off at the insults.

Planes began to crash into buildings and fields.

XXXI
Spike Takes Over

The world became agitated and afraid.

The Axe regained its color and perfect look when Spike picked it up. He chose to play sad. During his set buildings rained people.

Marshall was forced to observe each horror. All of the terrible and tragic things that were taking place that day were being showered upon him.

Marshall remained steadfast. The Preacher called for the next act.

XXXII
Serriana's Performance

Serriana ran through her many hits. Completely breaking their tradition of wearing all black, The Demimondaines sparkled brilliantly in virgin white costumes. They sang flawlessly.

"Okay, let's roll." Those words launched the counterattack on an airplane that crashed it into a Pennsylvania field close to a strip-mine.

In New Castle, a small city sixty-three miles north of Osgood, a freight train crushed a car sitting on the tracks with a whole family inside. Marshall watched all four of them get destroyed by the iron behemoth. Tears began to flood down Marshall's face. The preacher reached for the red flag. Marshall steeled up; the flag remained on the referee's belt.

Serriana counted into *Death of a Roadie.* All over the country the suicide rate spiked. Serriana's energy flagged. Waving his Bible, the referee signaled for her and the back-up singers to leave.

XXXIII
Last Song

Graham Graves did the most physical damage with his short set. As he strummed solo through the ever-changing *Last Song*, buildings collapsed within themselves.

God was certain that the bass player would stand up to watching those thousands of people each die. That was the deal. If Satan could crack Marshall and get him to beg to stop the assault on his senses, Evil would win. God knew this, or at least he thought he did. Doubt was new territory for God. There was a lot at stake. Next time I create a people, God pondered a bit, I might just leave that free will thing out.

XXXIV
Roadkillers Take It Out

It was Dog's turn. He was to deal out the shock and confusion that took over after the initial trauma ended.

Satan expected big returns from Dog's set.

The payoff was in lots of human pain and despair. The cards fell right and He got two or three long term wars out of it as well.

Satan was hot for Dog's woman, Cathy.

Normally Satan would just take her, but there was something about Dog that kept Him from doing it.

In reality the confrontation took years. The increase in gravity around the Axe interfered with time. To Marshall it all seem to pass in about six hours, the same length of time that God allowed his Son to hang on the Cross.

He just about caved when the train hit the car. The look of realized loss on the mother's face when she saw the locomotive racing furiously toward them was almost unbearable. There was no luxury of built-up callousness, each act caused him new pain.

Dog and Roadkillers continued to blast out their songs. It was days before the dust and debris stopped blowing around. People began to hang up pictures begging for information about lost loved ones. Some wanted revenge, some wanted forgiveness, all wanted to understand. Why?

New government agencies were hastily formed and given huge amounts of power. The people needed to be protected, so they necessarily lost some of their freedoms. The right to travel without restriction was severely impinged. Free speech suffered a few big dents as well.

One group blamed another group and Satan gained ground.

The bass player stayed fast. The tears he shed allowed him some relief from the amazing pressure. At one point the Axe took a decisive lead. Dog was ripping metal power chords on it, shaking the very foundation of Heaven.

Marshall continued to stand. If any sense could be made of this situation, Good had to survive.

XXXV
Most Wicked Bitch

Now Cathy was front and center. Gravestones on either side framed her standing behind the microphone. The congas and shakers began to play a familiar pattern. Then the piano struck a chord, at the same time Cathy began to sing in the purest of voice.

Let me introduce myself
I'm a woman of wealth and means...

Keith and Mick were stage left sharing a Shure 58 to sing back-up vocals. It sounded just like the recording. Marshall knew that they were still alive and figured they must have been there by special invitation.

In the background, just behind Buddy's kit, a thin milky white wall appeared. There were three men visible through it. The three stood apart and seemed unaware of each other. They also seemed completely unaware of the concert taking place before them in the cemetery.

Marshall could see them plainly and knew who they were. Three men, Judas, Adolph, and Martin. He understood that he was being shown Perdition. God was letting Marshall know where he was going to end up if he failed.

Really God, threats? I thought you loved me?

It kept getting worse. Person after person's life ended horribly in front of him. Some went down fighting hard, others quietly surrendered. Marshall could smell fear on almost all of them. Some seemed to be at peace with the inevitable.

There was a small percentage however, that ran toward it with joyful anticipation. Those few caused Marshall the greatest pain.

Life was precious. Why would someone want to willingly leave it behind?

Satan could not understand. He was sending the most terrible sights imaginable to Marshall, but Marshall did not bend or beg.

Satan's Guitar was failing to create enough emotional destruction to break the man.

XXXVI
The Decision

The referee made the call and signaled. It was over. He sent Roadkillers away and declared Good the winner. It was very close, but compassion finally tipped the scales toward Marshall.

Compassion was the one thing Satan and His bands lacked completely.

The Axe totally lost its power. As Dog made his exit, he dropped it to the ground. It was no longer under Satan's control.

Marshall's private Hell came to an end. The '63 Gibson ES-335 lay there at his feet, defeated and inert.

He felt much older than his sixty years. The cemetery's population had grown a lot during the time that Marshall stood there oblivious to the physical world. New stones and graves dotted the grounds. His suitcase and its contents were long gone. Parched and very tired, he hitched the bass guitar case up onto his shoulder and started back toward Osgood. He tried to whistle, but his mouth was way too dry.

Other things were new besides the graves. A small red building sat alongside the road fitted with a large diesel generator. It was not there when Marshall first came to the cemetery. A lot of gray satellite dishes were hanging on a tall tower mounted to a concrete slab. Thick black cables connected them to the building.

The boxy vehicle that passed him during the walk back to town was a Scion. He had never heard of that brand. On the bumper, a red, white, and blue sticker touted the Obama/Biden ticket.

A house now stood on the town line where an empty field had been before. Sprinklers scattered around the landscaping were showering the freshly planted grass seed. Marshall pulled one of the feeder hoses loose and drank his fill. He then held the nozzle over his head and soaked himself to the skin.

He was really glad to see The Damm Bakery still in business. The bass player slacked his hunger with frosted chocolate donuts and little cartons of cold milk.

It just so happened that a grave-site service took place that afternoon. This would be the last of the kin buried in the Foamer family plot. It was filled to capacity. The gravedigger carefully maneuvered the backhoe around the standing stones. He got off of the tractor and marked the edges. He didn't want to accidentally dig up any of the other Foamers.

An old beat to Hell guitar was lying face up on the lush grass. The gravedigger, curious as to how it got there, placed it on the seat of the backhoe. At the end of the work day, he took it home with him. A Google search of the serial number left him shocked. He was in possession of one of the most famous Gibson guitars ever made.

The owner of the Hard Rock Cafe in Seattle made the winning bid. He told the gravedigger that the ES-335 would have commanded another ten-thousand dollars if it were still in the original case. The gravedigger had no idea where that case was located.

They amplified each other's power, so God demanded that the Axe and its case be eternally separated.

He originally wanted them both completely destroyed, but Satan talked Him out of that. The guitar was allowed to survive as a souvenir of the conflict.

The case got tossed into a black hole and was compressed by the exponentially increasing gravity field until it became the size of nothing.

The Gibson ended up in downtown Seattle. It was prominently displayed in a glass case hanging on a wall in the Hard Rock Cafe. The month and year of its manufacture and the names of the three known owners were printed on a plaque.

Model / Gibson ES-335 semi-hollow body

Serial / 63666

Manufactured / November, 1963

Suggested retail price / $429.00 with case

Known owners /

Rusty Collins – Rock-and-Roll 1963–1967

Serriana – Country 1968–1975

Dog – Heavy Metal 1989–2000

XXXVII
And in the End

Even though the referee shut down the concert in the graveyard and ended the contest, the conflict between Good and Evil continues on.

The ripples from that day will endlessly pulsate through mankind's future with far reaching influence. They will stop only when the sun's nuclear furnace runs out of hydrogen and our benevolent star implodes. The plumes of plasma and radiation will shove this little planet out of its orbit. In a very short time, the Earth will become nothing more than a giant charcoal briquette.

XXXVIII
Shut Up, Buddy!

Buddy Rich's next assignment was with Conway Twitty.

Conway had made it to Heaven, and as a favor to God, he agreed to put Buddy in his rhythm section. The gig lasted for over a thousand years and nearly drove Buddy out of his mind.

THE END

Kat,

Thank you for encouraging me to complete this story. You are the best!

A. L. Williams